OPEN CITY

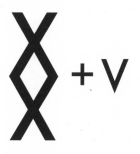

New York City, Summer 2008
Number Twenty-Five

 **OPEN CITY**

Actual Air
Poems by David Berman

"David Berman's poems are beautiful, strange, intelligent, and funny. They are narratives that freeze life in impossible contortions. They take the familiar and make it new, so new the reader is stunned and will not soon forget. I found much to savor on every page of *Actual Air*. It's a book for everyone."
—James Tate

"This is the voice I have been waiting so long to hear . . . Any reader who tunes in to his snappy, offbeat meditations is in for a steady infusion of surprises and delights."
—Billy Collins

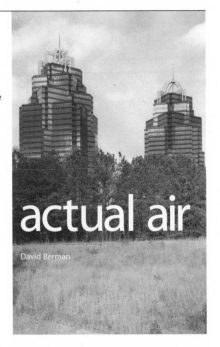

My Misspent Youth
Essays by Meghan Daum

"An empathic reporter and a provocative autobiographer . . . I finished it in a single afternoon, mesmerized and sputtering."
—*The Nation*

"Meghan Daum articulates the only secret left in the culture: discreet but powerful fantasies of romance, elegance, and ease that survive in our uncomfortable world of striving. These essays are very smart and very witty and just heartbreaking enough to be deeply pleasurable."
—Marcelle Clements

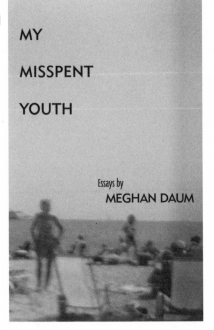

BOOKS

Open City Books are available at fine bookstores or at **www.opencity.org**, and are distributed to the trade by Publishers Group West.

Venus Drive
Stories by Sam Lipsyte

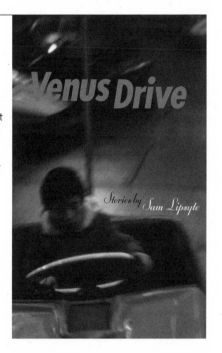

"Sam Lipsyte is a wickedly gifted writer. *Venus Drive* is filled with grimly satisfying fractured insights and hardcore humor. But it also displays some inspired sympathy for the daze and confusion of its characters. Above all it's wonderfully written and compulsively readable with brilliant and funny dialogue, a collection that represents the emergence of a very strong talent."
—Robert Stone

"Sam Lipsyte can get blood out of a stone—rich, red human blood from the stony sterility of contemporary life. His writing is gripping—at least I gripped this book so hard my knuckles turned white."
—Edmund White

Karoo
A Novel by Steve Tesich

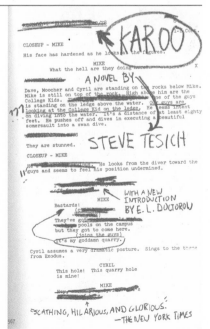

"Fascinating—a real satiric invention full of wise outrage."
—Arthur Miller

"A powerful and deeply disturbing portrait of a flawed, self-destructive, and compulsively fascinating figure."
—*Kirkus Reviews* (starred)

"Saul Karoo is a new kind of wild man, the sane maniac. Larger than life and all too human, his out-of-control odyssey through sex, death, and show business is extreme, and so is the pleasure of reading it. Steve Tesich created a fabulously Gargantuan comic character."
—Michael Herr

 **OPEN CITY**

Some Hope
A Trilogy by Edward St. Aubyn

"Tantalizing . . . A memorable tour de force."
—*The New York Times Book Review*

"Hilarious and harrowing by turns, sophisticated, reflective, and brooding."
—*The New York Review of Books*

"Feverishly good writing . . . Full of Algonquin wit on the surface while roiling underneath. *Some Hope* is a hell of a brew, as crisp and dry as a good English cider and as worth savoring as any of Waugh's most savage volleys."
—*The Ruminator Review*

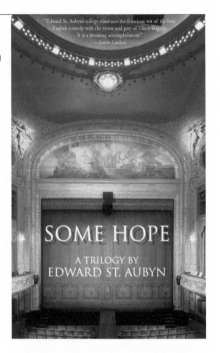

Mother's Milk
A Novel by Edward St. Aubyn

"St. Aubyn's caustic, splendid novel probes the slow violence of blood ties—a superbly realized agenda hinted at in the novel's arresting first sentence: 'Why had they pretended to kill him when he was born?'"
—*The Village Voice*

"Postpartum depression, assisted suicide, adultery, alcoholism—it's all here in St. Aubyn's keenly observed, perversely funny novel about an illustrious cosmopolitan family and the mercurial matriarch who rules them all."
—*People*

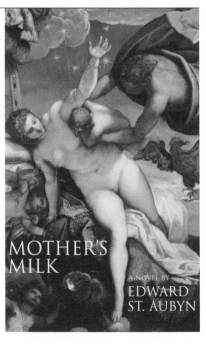

BOOKS

Goodbye, Goodness
A Novel by Sam Brumbaugh

"*Goodbye, Goodness* is the rock n' roll
Great Gatsby."
—New City Chicago

"Sam Brumbaugh's debut novel couldn't
be more timely. *Goodbye, Goodness*
boasts just enough sea air and action to
make an appealing summer read without coming anywhere near fluffsville."
—Time Out New York

"Beautifully captures the wrung-out feel
of a depleted American century."
—Baltimore City Paper

The First Hurt
Stories by Rachel Sherman

"Sherman's writing is sharp, hard, and
honest; there's a fearlessness in her
work, an I'm-not-afraid-to-say-this quality.
Because she knows that most of us
have thought the same but didn't have
the guts to say it."
—Boston Phoenix

"Rachel Sherman writes stories like splin-
ters: they get under your skin and stay
with you long after you've closed the
book. These haunting stories are both
wonderfully, deeply weird and unset-
tlingly familiar."
—Judy Budnitz

 # OPEN CITY

Long Live a Hunger to Feed Each Other
Poems by Jerome Badanes

"Reading Jerome Badanes's poems is not so much reading a voice from the heartfelt past as reading a poet whose work is very much alive and yet reflects a lost—and meaningful—age. He is one of our good souls; he is one of our poets. I treasure his work."
—Gerald Stern

"The best best book publishing story of the year."
—*Poetry*

World on Fire
by Michael Brownstein

"Bold and ambitious, *World on Fire* engages the great issues of the day, mixing the personal with the political, demanding attention be paid, continuing in the great tradition of Whitman, Ginsberg, and Pound. Here's a howl for the twenty-first century."
—Eric Schlosser, author of *Fast Food Nation*

"One of the most eloquent recent poetic works to cover the downsides of 'progress' and to cry out for a counterpunch against the manipulations of empire."
—*Publishers Weekly* (starred review)

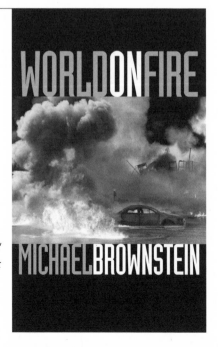

BOOKS

Love Without
Stories by Jerry Stahl

"[Stahl]…knows how to shock us into
laughter, and his best work mines the
grotesque for pathos, a tradition that
includes Flannery O'Connor, Barry
Hannah, and Denis Johnson . . .The key
isn't whom he writes about, but at what
depth . . . Stahl plunges us into depraved
worlds with a keen intensity of purpose,
and his addled protagonists run up hard
against the truth of their desires."
— *Los Angeles Times*

"Tender and gut-busting."
— *L.A. Weekly*

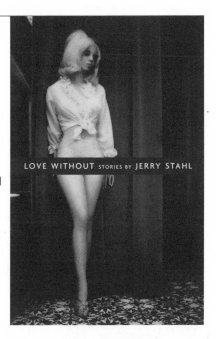

Why the Devil Chose New England for His Work
Stories by Jason Brown

"*Why the Devil Chose New England for
His Work* links gem-cut stories of troubled youths, alcoholics, illicit romances,
the burden of inheritance, and the bane
of class, all set in the dense upper
reaches of Maine, and delivers them
with hope, heart, and quiet humor."
— Lisa Shea, *Elle*

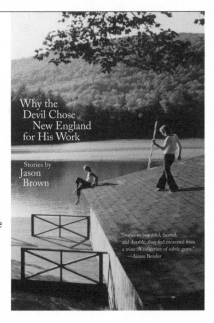

OPEN CITY BOOKS

FAREWELL
NAVIGATOR
STORIES BY LENI
ZUMAS

"Attention unrequited lovers, sisters of suicidal brothers, children of the legally blind: you are not alone. Leni Zumas understands your quiet agony and describes it with such a wry, unflinching familiarity that even the gory details ring true. If darkness has ever been your friend, your story is in here."
—Miranda July

"Zumas gives socially awkward, mysteriously gifted and self-destructive outcasts spellbinding, unflinching voice. . . . It's a powerful, irresistible collection."
    —*Publishers Weekly*

"Leni Zumas's writing is fearless and swift, sassy and sensational."
    —Joy Williams, author of *Honored Guest*

"I have never read stories like these before and I can't get them out of my head. Her language is real sorcery—it dismantles the world you think you know and takes you to strange, fecund territories of the imagination. Her characters are girls and boys in bad trouble, who feel as close to you and as far from you as the black sheep in your own family."
    —Karen Russell, author of *St. Lucy's Home for Girls Raised by Wolves*

OPEN CITY

LINCOLN PLAZA CINEMAS

Six Screens

63RD STREET & BROADWAY
OPPOSITE LINCOLN CENTER
212-757-2280

"A MAGNIFICENT FEAST OF STORYTELLING

bestowed upon one unlucky Bosnian town.
Sharp, funny, humane, and sometimes even magical."

—GARY SHTEYNGART, AUTHOR OF *ABSURDISTAN*

"[THE] VOICE OF A BOLD YOUNG EUROPE . . .

Brilliantly cockeyed prose that
borders on the surreal—
or maybe the psychedelic."

-LIBRARY JOURNAL (STARRED REVIEW)

"FUNNY AND HEARTFELT AND BRAZEN AND TRUE.

Find some space on your shelf beside
Aleksandar Hemon, Jonathan Safran
Foer, William Vollmann, and
David Foster Wallace."

—COLUM MCCANN, AUTHOR OF *ZOLI*

"The magic of storytelling lies at the heart
of Saša Stanišić's sensational debut. . . .

A BOOK THAT WILL DOMINATE THE DISCOURSE ON HOW CHILDREN EXPERIENCE WAR FOR A LONG TIME TO COME."

—*FOREIGN POLICY*

GROVE PRESS
an imprint of Grove/Atlantic, Inc.
Distributed by Publishers Group West

www.groveatlantic.com

OPEN CITY

Open City is published by Open City, Inc., a nonprofit corporation. Donations are tax-deductible to the extent allowed by the law. A one-year subscription (3 issues) is $30; a two-year subscription (6 issues) is $55. Make checks payable to: Open City, Inc., 270 Lafayette Street, Suite 1412, New York, NY 10012. For credit-card orders, see our Web site: www.opencity.org. E-mail: editors@opencity.org.

Open City is a member of the Council of Literary Magazines and Presses and is indexed by Humanities International Complete.

Open City gratefully acknowledges the generous support of the family of Robert Bingham. We also thank the New York State Council on the Arts and the Annenberg Foundation. See the page following the masthead for additional donor acknowledgments.

Front and back covers by Duncan Hannah. Front: *High Diver,* oil on canvas, 2005, collection of John Lambros. Back: *Monica Vitti*, pencil on paper, 2008.

Printed in the United States of America.
Copyright © 2008 by Open City, Inc.
All rights reserved.

ISBN-13: 978-1-890447-48-9
ISBN-10: 1-890447-48-X
ISSN: 1089-5523

OPEN CITY

EDITORS
Thomas Beller
Joanna Yas

ART DIRECTOR
Nick Stone

EDITOR-AT-LARGE
Adrian Dannatt

CONTRIBUTING EDITORS
Jonathan Ames
Elizabeth Beller
David Berman
Aimée Bianca
Jason Brown
Will Blythe
Sam Brumbaugh
Amanda Gersh
Patrick Gallagher
Laura Hoffmann
Jan de Jong
Kip Kotzen
Anthony Lacavaro
Alix Lambert
Vanessa Lilly
Sam Lipsyte
Jim Merlis
Honor Moore
Robert Nedelkoff
Parker Posey
Beatrice von Rezzori
Elizabeth Schmidt
Lee Smith
Alexandra Tager
Tony Torn
Jocko Weyland

INTERNS
Camille Perri
Ana Saldamando

READERS
Mike Gardner
Michael Hornburg
Jessa Lingel
Lina Makdisi
Rowland Miller
Aaron Rich

FOUNDING EDITORS
Thomas Beller
Daniel Pinchbeck

FOUNDING PUBLISHER
Robert Bingham

OPEN CITY WOULD LIKE TO THANK THE FOLLOWING FOR THEIR GENEROUS CONTRIBUTIONS

Patrons ($1,000 or more)
Clara Bingham
Joan Bingham
Belle & Henry Davis
Wendy Flanagan
Laura Hoffman
Alex Kuczynski
Vanessa & John Lilly
Eric Lindbloom & Nancy Willard
Eleanor & Rowland Miller
Scott Smith
Dorothy Spears
Mary & Jeffrey Zients

Donors ($500 or more)
Robert Scott Asen
Hava Beller
Holly Dando
Laura Fontana & John J. Moore
Nancy Novogrod
David Selig (Rice Restaurant)

Contributors ($150 or more)

Joe Andoe
Molly Bingham
Paula Bomer
Arlette P. Brauer & George Bria
Elizabeth Brown
Cheryl Chapman & Josh Gilbert
Nina Collins
Joe Conason & Elizabeth Wagley
Paula Cooper
E. V. Day and Ted Lee
Edward Garmey
Melissa Grace
Pierre Hauser
Edward Lee

Wendy Mullin
Richard & Nicole Murphy
Robert & René Nedelkoff
Miranda Lichtenstein &
    Cameron Martin
William Morton
Alexa Robinson & Steven Johnson
Rick Rofihe
Robert Soros &
    Melissa Schiff Soros
Georgia & Terry Stacey
Jennifer Sturman
Elizabeth Wagley & Joe Conason
Shelley Wanger

Friends

Alex Abramovich
Lucy Anderson
Harold Augenbraum
Caroline Baron
John Barr
Noah Baumbach
Elizabeth Beller
Jessica Bertel
Betsy Berne
Aimée Bianca
Andrew Blauner
Theodore Bouloukus
Sam Brumbaugh
Michael Carroll
Jocelyn Casey-Whitman
Bryan Charles
Winthrop Clevinger
Simon Constable
Hilary Metcalf Costa
Adrian Dannatt
Gerald Dillon
Sarah Dohrmann
Aaron Fagan
Mike Fellows
Jofie Ferrari-Adler
Nick Flynn
Tiffany Foa
Mike Gardner
Deborah Garrison
John Glassie
David Goodwillie
Melissa Gould
Rebecca Green
Gerald Howard
Amy Hundley

Brendan Kelly
Porochista Khakpour
Anthony Lacavaro
Deborah Landau
Matt Lee
Ariel Leve
Sam Lipsyte
Tzipora Lubar
Bruce Mason
Vestal McIntyre
Paul Morris
Carolyn Murnick
Christopher Nicholson
Ethan Nosowsky
Vince Passaro
Beatrice von Rezzori
Isabel Sadumi
Saïd Sayrafiezadeh
Elizabeth Schmidt
Richard Serra
Claudia Silver
Debra Singer
Betsy Smith
Joanna Spinks
Valerie Steiker
Ben Stiller
Nick Stone
Chaya Thanhauser
Ben Turner
Shawn Vandor
Marissa Walsh
Dean Wareham & Britta Phillips
Susan Wheeler
Zach Wiggin
Malerie Willens

Black
Clock

Aimee Bender · Tom Carson · Samuel R. Delany · Don DeLillo
Brian Evenson · Janet Fitch · Rebecca Goldstein · Maureen Howard
Shelly Jackson · Heidi Julavits · Miranda July · Jonathan Lethem
Ben Marcus · Greil Marcus · Rick Moody · Geoffrey O'Brien
Richard Powers · Joanna Scott · Darcey Steinke · Susan Straight
Lynne Tillman · David L. Ulin · Michael Ventura
William T. Vollmann · David Foster Wallace · Carlos Ruiz Zafon

Edited by Steve Erickson

Coming Soon Issue 9

www.blackclock.org • subscribe online

Published by CalArts in association with the MFA Writing Program

Photo Credit: Christopher Alexander, momentaryexistence.com

ANNA

CLOTHES FOR WOMEN

150 East 3rd Street at Avenue A
New York City
212.358.0195
www.annanyc.com

TWO DOCUMENTARIES

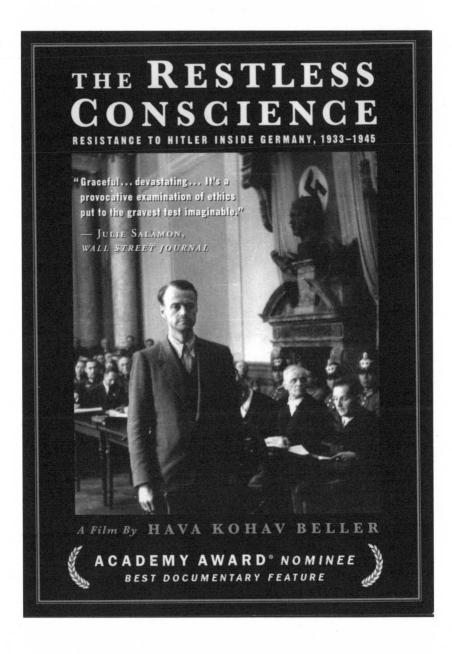

THE **RESTLESS CONSCIENCE**

RESISTANCE TO HITLER INSIDE GERMANY, 1933–1945

"Graceful... devastating... It's a provocative examination of ethics put to the gravest test imaginable."

— JULIE SALAMON,
WALL STREET JOURNAL

A Film By HAVA KOHAV BELLER

ACADEMY AWARD® NOMINEE
BEST DOCUMENTARY FEATURE

COMING SOON ON DVD

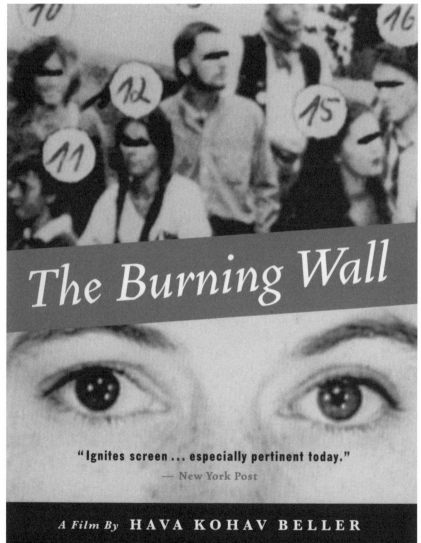

The Burning Wall

"Ignites screen ... especially pertinent today."
— New York Post

A Film By HAVA KOHAV BELLER

ACADEMY AWARD® NOMINEE for "The Restless Conscience" and
Recipient of THE COMMANDER'S CROSS OF THE ORDER OF MERIT

anderbo.com "Best New Online Journal"
—storySouth Million Writers Award

anderbo.com

fiction   poetry   "fact"   photography

RROfihe Trophy!

2007 Winner
Barbara Fillon

for her story
"The Peacock
(ten minutes in a bird's life)"

There were almost 200 stories submitted to the
2007 RRofihe Trophy Contest.

Barbara Fillon's story is published in this issue.
She will also receive $500 and a trophy.

2008 RRofihe Trophy Guidelines

- Stories should be typed, double-spaced, on 8 1/2 x 11 paper with the author's
  name and contact information on the first page and name and story title on the
  upper right corner of remaining pages.
- Submissions must be postmarked by September 15, 2008
- Limit one submission per author
- Author must not have been previously published in Open City
- Mail submissions to RRofihe, 270 Lafayette Street, Suite 1412, New York, NY 10012
- Enclose self addressed stamped business envelope to receive names of winner
  and honorable mentions
- All manuscripts are non-returnable and will be recycled.
- Reading fee is $10. Check or money order payable to RRofihe
- Judged by Rick Rofihe; 2008 Contest Assistant: Carolyn Wilsey

www.opencity.org/rrofihe

NEW YORK UNIVERSITY   Arts and Science

Writers in New York

June 2–26, 2008

Eight undergraduate credits

Writers in New York offers poets and fiction writers an opportunity to develop their craft while living the writer's life in Greenwich Village. Students participate in daily workshops and craft classes, are mentored by accomplished professional writers, and attend readings and talks by acclaimed New York-based writers and editors. Students in the program work intensively to generate new writing, study great literary works by other writers, and participate in a lively series of readings, lectures, literary walking tours, and special events, including *The Paris Review* Summer Salon.

FACULTY

George Foy (*Fiction Writing Workshop*)
Matthew Rohrer (*Poetry Craft Seminar*)
Helen Schulman (*Fiction Writing Workshop*)
Brenda Shaughnessy (*Poetry Writing Workshop*)
Irini Spanidou (*Fiction Craft Seminar*)
Joanna Yas (*Associate Director*)
Deborah Landau (*Director*)

VISITING WRITERS & EDITORS

David Baker, Joshua Beckman, Thomas Beller, Dan Chiasson, Chris Cox, Lydia Davis, Nick Flynn, Bonnie Friedman, Keith Gessen, Edward Hirsch, Radhika Jones, Yusef Komunyakaa, J. Robert Lennon, Sam Lipsyte, Meghan O'Rourke, Nathaniel Rich, Saïd Sayrafiezadeh, Rachel Sherman, Darin Strauss, Matt Weiland, Monica Youn, Matthew Zapruder and more

FIGHTING AIDS ONE BOOK AT A TIME

"One of the hottest literary hubs in New York: the bookstore salon that the city has been missing." – *The New York Times*

126 Crosby St.
(between Houston and Prince Streets)
New York, New York 10012
(212) 334-3324
www.housingworksbookstore.org
Monday-Friday, 10-9; Saturday, 12-7, Sunday, 12-7

HOUSING WORKS BOOKSTORE CAFE

CONTRIBUTORS' NOTES

HOWARD ALTMANN is a poet and playwright living in New York City. His first book of poems, *Who Collects the Days*, was published in 2005.

JONATHAN AMES is the author of the novels *I Pass Like Night*, *The Extra Man*, and *Wake Up, Sir!*, and the essay collections *My Less than Secret Life*, *What's Not to Love?*, and *I Love You More than You Know*. His graphic novel, *The Alcoholic*, with artwork by Dean Haspiel, will be published this fall by DC Comics. *The Double Life Is Twice as Good: Essays* is forthcoming in 2009 from Scribner.

CHARLES BUKOWSKI was born in Anderbach, Germany in 1920 and grew up in Los Angeles. He published more than forty-five books of poetry and prose, including *Legs, Hips, and Behind*; *Post Office*, *Barfly*, and *Notes of a Dirty Old Man*. He died in 1994 in San Pedro, California. The piece in this issue will appear in *Portions from a Wine-Stained Notebook: Uncollected Poems and Essays 1944–1990*, edited by David Calonne, forthcoming from City Lights in the fall.

MARK C is a New York City–based musician and photographer. He is a founding member of the postpunk bands Live Skull and Spoiler. He sings and plays guitar in International Shades, whose second album *Luv & Terror* will be released in August on Gifted Children Records. His photographs have been featured on several album covers, including Live Skull's *Dusted* and Sugar's *Copper Blue*.

BARBARA FILLON grew up in Tennessee, earned a BA in English literature at the University of Chicago, and now lives in New York City.

RIVKA GALCHEN grew up in Norman, Oklahoma, the child of Israeli immigrants. She attended Princeton and went on to get her MD at Mount Sinai School of Medicine. Galchen was a Robert Bingham Fellow and Writing Instructor Fellow at Columbia's MFA program, has been published in *The New Yorker*, *Zoetrope*, and *Harper's*, and was awarded a 2006 Rona Jaffe Foundation Writers Award. Her debut novel, *Atmospheric Disturbances*, will be published by Farrar, Straus and Giroux this spring.

JON GROEBNER lives in Seattle with his wife and son and daughter. He is writing a novel.

DUNCAN HANNAH is a Manhattan-based painter who has had over forty solo exhibitions since his debut in 1981. His work is in the permanent collections of the Metropolitan Museum of Art and the Chicago Art Institute. He is represented by James Graham & Sons.

ELLEN HARVEY was born in Kent, England and lives in New York City. Her work has recently been exhibited at Luxe Gallery, Magnus Müller (Berlin), and the 2008 Whitney Biennial.

GIUSEPPE O. LONGO holds degrees in mathematics and electronic engineering and is professor of Information Theory at the University of Trieste, Italy. His real love, however, is literature, which, as he says, "has saved him from reductionism." He has published three novels, eight collections of short stories, and a collection of plays. His work has received a variety of awards and prizes and has been translated from Italian into French, German, Portuguese, Russian, and now English.

JAMES B. MICHELS is a native of Michigan. He has a PhD in literature and has published critical articles on James Joyce, Roland Barthes, and Yves Bonnefoy. He teaches Italian language and culture at Wayne State University in Detroit.

JOHN O'CONNOR is from Kalamazoo, Michigan. His writing has appeared in *Quarterly West, The Believer, Gastronomica, The Financial Times*, and *The Best Creative Nonfiction 2006*. He lives in New York City.

JENNIFER RICHTER is a former Wallace Stegner Fellow and Jones Lecturer in Poetry at Stanford University. Her poems have appeared in many publications, including *Poetry, Ploughshares, Crab Orchard Review*, and *The Healing Muse*.

SAID SHIRAZI lives in suburban New Jersey. His fiction has recently appeared in *Fifth Wednesday* and is forthcoming in *Ninth Letter*. He also writes about music and TV for the online journal *Printculture*.

MICHAEL SCOGGINS was born in Washington D.C. and grew up in Virginia. He received his MFA in painting from the Savannah College of Art and Design. He lives and works in Brooklyn, and has gallery representation in Atlanta, Miami, New York, San Francisco, and Vienna.

ROBERT STONE is the acclaimed author of seven novels, including *A Hall of Mirrors* (winner of the National Book Award), *A Flag for Sunrise, Children of Light, Outerbridge Reach, Damascus Gate*, and *Bay of Souls*, and the nonfiction work *Prime Green: Remembering the Sixties*. His short-story collection, *Bear and His Daughter*, was a finalist for the Pulitzer Prize. The recipient of a Guggenheim Fellowship, Stone lives with his wife in New York City.

BEN CARLTON TURNER was born in Walnut Creek, California. He has been published in *The Believer, Salt Hill*, and others. Longer works include a chapbook entitled *The Death of Good Sailor Bob*. He lives and works in New York City and is currently completing a novel.

SARAH BORDEN WARECK holds an MFA from the Warren Wilson Program for Writers. Her story collection, *East Side Stories*, was a semifinalist for the 2007 Sarabande Books Mary McCarthy Prize Contest, judged by Mary Gaitskill. Her work has appeared in several journals, including *Willow Springs, Beloit Fiction Journal, Chicago Reader, Other Voices*. She lives with her two daughters in New Haven and is working on a novel.

PRAISE FOR post road

"Post Road, from its inception, has been an exotic and intelligent literary treat. I always like to see what they come up with each issue, and they never fail to surprise, entertain, and enlighten."

JONATHAN AMES, AUTHOR OF *WAKE UP, SIR!*

"I always read *Post Road* with great enthusiasm. In its stealthy, unassuming way, it has become one of the most reliable and ambitious literary magazines in America."

RICK MOODY, AUTHOR OF *DEMONOLOGY*

"*Post Road* is one of the most interesting and exciting literary magazines out there. If you care about reading and writing, do yourself a favor and check it out."

TOM PERROTTA, AUTHOR OF *LITTLE CHILDREN*

"*Post Road* maps the way to the freshest and funkiest literary territories. As the group The Postal Service does for music, *Post Road* fuses eclectic elements into something whole and wholly new."

ELIZABETH SEARLE, AUTHOR OF *CELEBRITIES IN DISGRACE*

"The editors' enthusiasm is palpable; they consistently provide a lively home for writing worth reading."

AMY HEMPEL, AUTHOR OF *TUMBLE HOME*

"Post Road has the goods. I not only read fall on them and read them like hot news when they come in the door, I keep them lined up on my shelf like little books, because that's what they are."

JONATHAM LETHEM, AUTHOR OF *FORTRESS OF SOLITUDE*

1 YEAR: $18, 2 YEARS: $34 **WWW.POSTROADMAG.COM**

ARTCRITICISMFICTIONNONFICTIONPOETRYTHEATREETCETERARECOMMENDATIONS

*The editors would like to congratulate the following
Open City contributors for their recent honors*

Best American Essays 2008
"Where God Is Glad" by Joe Wenderoth (from *Open City* #23)

Best Creative Nonfiction 2008
"My First Fairy Tale" by Vijay Seshadri (from *Open City* #23)

2008 Whitney Biennial
Matthew Brannon
Roe Ethridge
Ellen Harvey
Karen Kilimnick
Mungo Thomson

2008 Guggenheim Fellow
Sam Lipsyte

2007 National Book Award
Denis Johnson

2007 National Book Award "5 Under 35" Selection
Dinaw Mengestu

2007 National Book Critics Circle Award Finalist
Matthea Harvey

2008 Academy of Arts & Letters Award in Literature
Will Eno
Fanny Howe

2008 Academy of Arts & Letters
Harold D. Vursell Memorial Award
Maxine Swann

RICE

NEW LOCATION

292 ELIZABETH ST
N O H O
212-226-5775

RICENY.COM

NICK STONE DESIGN

www.nickstonedesign.com
stone@nickstonedesign.com
tel: 212.995.1863

OPEN

"The Crazy Person" by Mary Gaitskill, "La Vie en Rose" by Hubert Selby Jr., "Cathedral Parkway" by Vince Passaro. Art by Jeff Koons and Devon Dikeou. Cover by Ken Schles, whose *Invisible City* sells for thousands on Ebay. Stan Friedman's poems about baldness and astronomy, Robert Polito on Lester Bangs, Jon Tower's real life letters to astronauts. (Vastly underpriced at $300. Only three copies left.)

A first glimpse of Martha McPhee; a late burst from Terry Southern. Jaime Manrique's "Twilight at the Equator." Art by Paul Ramirez-Jonas, Kate Milford, Richard Serra. Kip Kotzen's "Skate Dogs," Richard Foreman's "Poetry City" with playful illustrations by Daniel Pinchbeck, David Shields' "Sports" and his own brutal youth. (Ken Schles found the negative of our cover girl on Thirteenth Street and Avenue B. We're still looking for the girl. $25)

Irvine Welsh's "Eurotrash" (his American debut), Richard Yates (from his last, unfinished novel), Patrick McCabe (years before *The Butcher Boy*). Art by Francesca Woodman (with an essay by Betsy Berne), Jacqueline Humphries, Allen Ginsberg, Alix Lambert. A short shot of Lipsyte—"Shed"—not available anywhere else. Plus Alfred Chester's letters to Paul Bowles. Chip Kidd riffs on the Fab Four. (Very few copies left! $25)

Stories by the always cheerful Cyril Connolly ("Happy Deathbeds"), Thomas McGuane, Jim Thompson, Samantha Gillison, Michael Brownstein, and Emily Carter, whose "Glory Goes and Gets Some" was reprinted in *Best American Short Stories.* Art by Julianne Swartz and Peter Nadin. Poems by David Berman and Nick Tosches. Plus Denis Johnson in Somalia. (A monster issue, sales undercut by slightly rash choice of cover art by editors. Get it while you can! $15)

Change or Die
Stories by David Foster Wallace, Siobhan Reagan, Irvine Welsh. Jerome Badanes' brilliant novella, "Change or Die" (film rights still available). Poems by David Berman and Vito Acconci. Plus Helen Thorpe on the murder of Ireland's most famous female journalist, and Delmore Schwartz on T. S. Eliot's squint. (Still sold-out! Wait for e-books to catch on or band together and demand a reprint.)

CITY back issues

Make an investment in your future...
In today's volatile marketplace
you could do worse.

The Only Woman He's Ever Left
Stories by James Purdy, Jocko Weyland, Strawberry Saroyan. Michael Cunningham's "The Slap of Love." Poems by Rick Moody, Deborah Garrison, Monica Lewinsky, Charlie Smith. Art by Matthew Ritchie, Ellen Harvey, Cindy Stefans. Rem Koolhaas project. With a beautiful cover by Adam Fuss. (Only $10 for this blockbuster.)

ISSUE #6

The Rubbed Away Girl
Stories by Mary Gaitskill, Bliss Broyard, and Sam Lipsyte. Art by Jimmy Raskin, Laura Larson, and Jeff Burton. Poems by David Berman, Elizabeth Macklin, Stephen Malkmus, and Will Oldham. (We found some copies in the back of the closet so were able to lower the price! $25 (it *was* $50))

ISSUE #7

Beautiful to Strangers
Stories by Caitlin O'Connor Creevy, Joyce Johnson, and Amine Wefali, back when her byline was Zaitzeff (now the name of her organic sandwich store at Nassau & John Streets—go there for lunch!). Poems by Harvey Shapiro, Jeffrey Skinner, and Daniil Kharms. Art by David Robbins, Liam Gillick, and Elliott Puckette. Piotr Uklanski's cover is a panoramic view of Queens, shot from the top of the World Trade Center in 1998. ($10)

ISSUE #8

Bewitched
Stories by Jonathan Ames, Said Shirazi, and Sam Lipsyte. Essays by Geoff Dyer and Alexander Chancellor, who hates rabbit. Poems by Chan Marshall, Lucy Anderson, and Edvard Munch on intimate and sensitive subjects. Art by Karen Kilimnick, Giuseppe Penone, Mark Leckey, Maurizio Cattelan, and M.I.M.E. (Oddly enough, our bestselling issue. ($10))

ISSUE #9

Editors' Issue
Previously demure editors publish themselves. Enormous changes at the last minute. Stories by Robert Bingham, Thomas Beller, Daniel Pinchbeck, Joanna Yas, Adrian Dannatt, Kip Kotzen, Geoffrey O'Brien, Lee Smith, Amanda Gersh, and Jocko Weyland. Poems by Tony Torn. Art by Nick Stone, Meghan Gerety, and Alix Lambert. (Years later, Ken Schles's cover photo appears on a Richard Price novel.) ($10)

ISSUE #10

OPEN

Octo Ate Them All
Vestal McIntyre emerges from the slush pile like aphrodite with a brilliant story that corresponds to the tattoo that covers his entire back. Siobhan Reagan thinks about strangulation. Fiction by Melissa Pritchard and Bill Broun. Anthropologist Michael Taussig's Cocaine Museum. Gregor von Rezzori's meditation on solitude, sex, and raw meat. Art by Joanna Kirk, Sebastien de Ganay, and Ena Swansea. ($10)

Equivocal Landscape
Sam Brumbaugh, author of *Goodbye, Goodness*, debuts with a story set in Kenya, Daphne Beal and Swamiji, Paula Bomer sees red on a plane, Heather Larimer hits a dog, and Hunter Kennedy on the sexual possibilities of Charlottesville versus West Texas. Ford Madox Ford on the end of fun. Poetry by Jill Bialosky and Rachel Wetzsteon. Art by Miranda Lichtenstein and Pieter Schoolwerth; a love scene by Toru Hayashi. Mungo Thomson passes notes. ($10)

Hi-fi
Sam Lipsyte introduces Steve. Nick Tosches smokes with God. Jack Walls remembers the gangs of Chicago. Vince Passaro ponders adult content. Poetry by Honor Moore, Sarah Gorham, and Melissa Holbrook Pierson. Mini-screenplay by Terry Southern. Art by Luisa Kazanas, Peter Pinchbeck, and Julianne Swartz. Special playwrighting section guest edited by Tony Torn. ($10)

Something Like Ten Million
The defacto life and death issue. Amazing debut stories from Nico Baumbach, Michiko Okubo, and Sarah Porter; Craig Chester writes on why he has the face he deserves; a bushy, funny, and phallic art project from Louise Belcourt. Special poetry section guest edited by Lee Ann Brown. A photo essay of fleeing Manhattanites by Ken Schles. The cover is beautiful and weird, a bright hole in downtown Manhattan. ($10)

That Russian Question
Another excerpt from Amine Wefali's *Westchester Burning (see Open City #8)*. Alicia Erian in *Jeopardy*. Jocko Weyland does handplants for an audience of elk. James Lasdun on travel and infidelity. Lara Vapnyar's debut publication. Poetry by Steve Healy, Daniel Nester, Lev Rubinshtein, and Daniel Greene. ($10)

CITY

Please send a check or
money order payable to:

Open City, Inc.
270 Lafayette Street, Suite 1412
New York, NY 10012

For credit-card orders, see www.opencity.org.

I wait, I wait.
A brilliant outtake from Robert Bingham's *Lightning on the Sun*. Ryan Kenealy on the girl who ran off with the circus; Nick Tosches on Proust. Art by Allen Ruppersberg, David Bunn, Nina Katchadourian, Matthew Higgs, and Matthew Brannon. Stories by Evan Harris, Lewis Robinson, Michael Sledge, and Bruce Jay Friedman. Rick Rofihe feels Marlene. Poetry by Dana Goodyear, Nathaniel Bellows, and Kevin Young. ($10)

They're at it again.
Lara Vapnyar's "There Are Jews in My House," Chuck Kinder on Dagmar. Special poetry section guest edited by Honor Moore, including C. K. Williams, Victoria Redel, Eamon Grennan, and Carolyn Forché. Art by Stu Mead, Christoph Heemann, Jason Fox, Herzog film star Bruno S., and Sophie Toulouse, whose "Sexy Clowns" project has become a "character note for [our] intentions" (says the *Literary Magazine Review*). See what all the fuss is about. ($10)

I Want to Be Your Shoebox
Susan Chamandy on Hannibal's elephants and hockey, Mike Newirth's noirish "Semiprecious." Rachel Blake's "Elephants" (an unintentional elephant theme emerges). Poetry by Catherine Bowman and Rodney Jack. Art by Viggo Mortensen, Alix Lambert, Marcellus Hall, Mark Solotroff, and Alaskan Pipeline polar bear cover by Jason Middlebrook (we're still trying to figure out what the bear had for lunch). ($10)

Post Hoc Ergo Propter Hoc
Stories by Jason Brown, Bryan Charles, Amber Dermont, Luis Jaramillo, Dawn Raffel, Bryan Charles, Nina Shope, and Alicia Erian. Robert Olen Butler's severed heads. Poetry by Jim Harrison, Sarah Gorham, Trevor Dannatt, Matthew Rohrer & Joshua Beckman, and Harvey Shapiro. Art by Bill Adams, Juliana Ellman, Sally Ross, and George Rush. Eerie, illustrated children's story by Rick Rofihe and Thomas Roberston. Saucy cover by Wayne Gonzales. ($10)

Homecoming
"The Egg Man" a novella by Scott Smith, author of *A Simple Plan* (screenplay and book); Ryan Kenealy does God's math; an unpublished essay by Paul Bowles. Stories by Rachel Sherman, Sam Shaw, and Maxine Swann. Art by Shelter Serra, William McCurtin (of *Story of My Scab* and *Elk* fame). Poems by Anthony Roberts, Honor Moore, and David Lehman. ($10)

OPEN CITY

back issues

Ballast
Matthew Zapruder's "The Pajamaist," David Nutt's "Melancholera," fiction by Rachel Sherman, a Nick Tosches poem, Phillip Lopate's "Tea at the Plaza," David A. Fitschen on life on tour as a roadie. Poetry by Matt Miller and Alex Phillips. Art by Molly Smith, Robert Selwyn, Miranda Lichtenstein, Lorenzo Petrantoni, Billy Malone, and M Blash. ($10)

Fiction/Nonfiction
A special double-sided issue featuring fiction by Sam Lipsyte, Jerry Stahl, Herbert Gold, Leni Zumas, Matthew Kirby, Jonathan Baumbach, Ann Hillesland, Manuel Gonzales, and Leland Pitts-Gonzales. Nonfiction by Priscilla Becker, Vestal McIntyre, Eric Pape, Jocko Weyland, and Vince Passaro. ($10)

Prose by Poets
Prose and poetry by Anne Sexton, Nick Flynn, Jim Harrison, Wayne Koestenbaum, Joe Wenderoth, Glyn Maxwell, Rebecca Wolff, Vijay Seshadri, Jerome Badanes, Deborah Garrison, Jill Bialosky, Cynthia Kraman, Max Blagg, Thorpe Moeckel, Greg Purcell, Rodney Jack, Hadara Bar-Nadav, and Nancy Willard. ($10)

Secret Engines
Three debuts: Malerie Willens, Gerard Coletta, and Ian Martin. Stanley Moss as a bronze satyr; heavy breathing with Jeff Johnson. Stories by Jonathan Baumbach, Erin Brown, Wayne Conti, James Hannaham, and Claire Keegan. Poetry by Mark Hartenbach, Alex Lemon, and Baron Wormser. Art by Amy Bird, Jay Batlle, Noelle Tan, and Doug Shaeffer. ($10)

SUBSCRIBE

One year (3 issues) for $30; two years (6 issues) for $55.
Add $10/year for Canada & Mexico; $20/year for all other countries.

Please send a check or money order payable to:
Open City, Inc.   270 Lafayette Street, Suite 1412   New York, NY 10012
For credit-card orders, see www.opencity.org.

The city has a thousand stories...What's yours?
Tell your New York stories

www.mrbellersneighborhood.com

Attention Teachers:

Mapsites.net is a web based teaching tool that allows students to post historical presentations, personal essays, and creative writing onto an interactive map of their neighborhood.

Mapsites.net is ideal for American History and Urban history courses, as well as English courses in which creative writing or personal essay composition, or even photography, play a role. Any class which encourages students to think about their physical environment in terms of the past or the present could make excellent use of Mapsites.

www.mapsites.net

High Wire

Robert Stone

I FIRST MET LUCY AT A MOVIE PREMIERE AT GRAUMAN'S ABOUT midway between the death of Elvis Presley and the rise of Bill Clinton. Attending was a gesture of support for the director, who happened to be a friend of mine. The film's distributors had made a halfhearted lurch toward an old-style Grauman's opening, breaking out a hastily dyed red carpet. A couple of searchlights swept the murky night sky over downtown Hollywood. By then these occasions were exhausted flickers of the past, so there were none of the much-parodied rituals some of us watched in black-and-white newsreels at the corner Bijou. No more flashbulbs or narrators with society lockjaw telling us what the talent was wearing. Neither simpering interviewers nor doomed starlets walking the walk. The camera flashes and the demented fans crowding the velvet rope were all memories. Hollywood Boulevard was even rattier then than it is now. The only people around the marquee that night were frightened-looking Japanese tourists and bright-eyed street freaks with slack smiles.

The picture was no good. It was the forced sequel to a 1960s hit with a plot cribbed from a John Ford movie of the fifties. It featured two very old actors, revered figures from the time of legend, and the point of it was the old dears' opportunity to recycle their best beloved shtick. The withered couple and its more agile doubles shuffled through outdoor adventures and a heartwarming geriatric romance stapled to some bits of fossil Western. Attempts had been made to make it all contemporary with winks and nods and brain-dead ironizing.

The audience consisted mainly of people who were there on assignment, out of politeness, or from fear. There were also members of the moviegoing public, admitted by coupons available through the homes-of-celebrities tours and at the cashier counters of cheap restaurants. Raven-haired Lucy, with her throaty voice and dark-eyed Armenian fire, was actually in the picture briefly, as an Apache maid. I later learned she was not in the theater to take pleasure in the picture or even in her own performance. She had come in the service of romance, her own, involving an alcoholic, Heathcliffish British actor, the movie's villain.

Heathcliff had made Lucy crazy that night by escorting his handsome and chic wife, suddenly reunited with her husband and relocated from London. It seemed that the sight of them had stricken her physically; when I saw her sitting alone a few seats down from me she was cringing tearfully in the darks and lights from the screen.

My first impulse was to leave her alone in her distress. I was certainly not impelled to a hypocritical display of concern. But it was one of those bells; I was unattached, still single, due to leave town in a week. Maybe I'd had a drink or smoked a joint before the appalling show. Anyway I moved one seat toward her.

"Nice scenery," I said.

She looked at me in a flash of the big sky country's exterior daylight, removing her stylish glasses to dab at her tears and sitting upright in her seat.

"Oh, thanks."

Her tone was predictably one of annoyed sarcasm but I chose not to interpret it as the blowing off she intended. Sometimes you can parse a hasty word in the semi-dark and I decided not to be discouraged, at least not so quickly. I realized then that she had some connection with the picture on the screen. An actress, a production girl?

In those days I was confident to the point of arrogance. I assumed I was growing more confident with time. How could I know that the more you knew the more troubled and cautious you became, that introspection cut your speed and endurance? We watched for a while and she shifted in her seat and touched her hair. I interpreted these as favorable portents and moved over to a place one seat away from her. At that distance I recognized her among the film's cast. Scarcely a minute later on screen, Brion Pritchard, her real-life deceiver, callously gunned down her character, the Apache soubrette. I watched her witness the tearjerky frames of her own death scene. She appeared unmoved, stoical, and grim.

"Good job," I said.

Lucy fidgeted, turned to me, and spoke in a stage whisper that must have been audible three rows away.

"She sucked!" Lucy declared, distancing herself from the performance and turning such scorn on the hapless young indigen that I winced.

"So let's go," I suggested.

Lucy was reluctant to go, afraid of being spotted by our mutual friend the director who had also produced the film. She expected to look to him for employment before long. However, she seemed to find being hit on a consolation. It was the first glimpse I had of her exhausting impulsiveness.

We sneaked out in a crouch like two stealthy movie Indians, under cover of a darkness dimly lighted by a day for night sequence. The two stars on screen told each other their sad backstories by a campfire. Their characters had the leisure to chat because Apaches never attacked at night.

Across the street, appropriately, a country and western hat band from Kyoto was crooning rural melodies. The two of us jaywalked across Hollywood and into the lobby of the fading hotel where the band was performing. A man in a stained tuxedo—an unwelcoming figure—directed us to a table against one wall. I ordered a Pacifico; Lucy had Pellegrino and a Valium.

"It's Canada," Lucy told me.

"What is?"

"The scenery. In the thing over there."

"The thing? You don't remember what the picture's called?"

"I like repressed it," she said and gritted her teeth. "Sure I know what it's called. It had different titles post-production."

"Such as?"

"*Unbound. Unleashed. Uncooked.*"

We introduced ourselves and claimed we had heard of each other. For a while we watched the hat act sing and swing. The lads looked formidable under their tilted sombreros. Their lead singer sang lyrics phonetically, rendering interpretations of "I Can't Stop Loving You," "I'm Walking the Floor," and other favorites. Their audience was scant and boozy. There were a few other bold escapees from the premier across the street.

"You were a great Apache."

She only shook her head. Plainly even qualified professional regard would take us nowhere. For some reason I persisted.

"Come on, I was moved. You dying. Featured role."

"Dying is easy," she said. "Ever hear that one?"

I had. It was an old actor's joke about the supposed last words of Boris Thomashevsky, an immortal of the Yiddish stage. Surrounded by weeping admirers seeking to comfort him, he gave them a farewell message. "Dying is easy," said the old man. "Comedy is hard."

"They shot different endings," Lucy explained. "One sad, one happy."

"Really?" It was hard to believe they would perpetrate a sad ending with the two beloveds, which would only have made a fatuous movie even worse. When riding a turkey, I believe, cleave to the saddle horn of tradition. But sad endings were a new thing in those years—the era of the worst movies ever made. Industry supremos who hadn't been on the street unaccompanied for forty years were still trying to locate the next generation of dimwits. So they tried sad endings and dirty words and nude body doubles. There was no more production code, movies were supposed to get serious and adult. Sad endings were as close as most of them could reach.

"So I hear. I wasn't there. I didn't read the endings. Like I had other things on my mind. I didn't see it, did I? We're over here."

"O.K."

"I bet they went with the happy though." She sneaked a quick look around and bit a half of her second ten-gram Valium. I told her the happy seemed likely.

"Oh," she said, and she smiled for the first time in our acquaintance, "Tom Loving. You're a writer." She either guessed or actually had somehow heard of me. Her smile was appropriately sympathetic.

She told me they had reshot a lot during the filming, different versions of different scenes.

"I die in all of them," she said.

Eventually we drove our separate cars to an anchored trailer she was renting on the beach in Malibu. As I remember, she was tooling around in a big Jaguar XJ6. We sat under her wind-tattered awning on the trailer's oceanfront deck and a west wind peeled wisps of cold, briny fog off the ocean. It was refreshing after the sickly perfume of the theater and the haze of booze and smoke in the lounge.

"I'm not happy." Lucy told me. "I'm sure you could tell, right?"

"I saw you were crying. I thought it was over the movie."

"If we'd stayed," she said, "you would have cried too."

"Was it that bad?"

"Yes," she said. "Yes! It was deeply bad. And on top of it that bastard Pritchard whom I've always loved." She looked at me thoughtfully for a moment. "You know?"

"I do," I said. "We've all been there."

She looked away and laughed bitterly, as though her lofty grief must be beyond the limits of my imagination. I was annoyed since I had hoped to divert her from pining. On the other hand, it was entertaining to watch her doing unrequited love with restraint and a touch of self-scorning irony.

"This man is deliberately trying to make me crazy," she said. "And to kill himself."

"It's a type," I explained.

"Oh yeah?" She gave me another pitying glance. "You think so?"

She had crushed my helpful routine. I put it aside. "Was that the wife?" I asked. "The blonde?"

"Yes," Lucy said. "Think she's attractive?"

"Well," I said, "on a scale of yes or no. . . ."

"All right, all right," she said. "All right."

"Met her?"

"I have met her," said Lucy. "When I did I thought hey, she's not a bad kid. But she's a fucking bitch it turns out."

I kept my advice to myself and little by little Lucy detached herself from her regrets. Later I came to know how suddenly her moods could change. It was of course an affliction, in her case untreatable. She kept her ghosts close at hand and always on call. They were present as a glimmer of surprise that never disappeared behind her eyes.

After a while I got her to walk with me; we shed our shoes and went across the moonlit beach. Brion seemed to be off her mind.

The sand at the water's edge had a steep drop-off to the surf. We clambered down to the wet sand where the waves broke. The sea's withdrawing force was nearly enough to pull us off our feet. Lucy lost her balance and I had to put an arm around her waist to preserve her.

"It could take you away," Lucy said.

We had a hard time climbing the four feet or so to the looser sand, hard enough to leave us out of breath. As we walked back, Lucy told a story from her earliest days in town. She had fallen in with some fast-lane hipsters. Many of them came from industry families. One night she and a friend found themselves on the beach with the daughter of a world-famous entertainment figure. The daughter passed out on the sand, so when Lucy and her friend saw somebody coming they ran off into the nearby shadows. Two men arrived, equally world famous. They encountered the daughter sprawled on the sand and tried to rouse her. The adolescent had responded with dazed, rude mutterings. One man told the other whose daughter she was. Lucy always remembered his Viennese accent.

"Ja," the man said to his friend. "Kid's a valking disaster."

Lucy and her friend giggled in the dark. Who could walk?

"I don't drink anymore," Lucy told me.

In spite of her solemn reflections, when we got back to the trailer she produced some quaaludes and cocaine for me. I did a sopor and a couple of lines on her beautiful goatskin table. We drank champagne with it, which I feared would be a mistake. We were ready to get it on, both of us, but I wondered briefly if she might not suffer a morning after the fact change of heart. She was a woman on the rebound, I was a stranger and I was afraid there might be recriminations. That was not Lucy but I didn't know it then. She seemed so mercurial. I think we watched a little of Carson that night and found it uproariously funny in the wrong places. It was true that she smoked incessantly and smelled of tobacco. Otherwise she was a Levantine angel, one of the celestial damsels awarded to the devout and to me. In the sack she told me about her early life in Fresno.

"Know what people called Armenians?" she asked.

"What, baby?" We had gone to bed to Otis Redding, "Dock of the Bay," and there beside me Lucy addressed her après cigarette with such intensity and style that, after three years clean, I wanted one too. "Tell me what they called the poor Armenians?"

"They called us the Fresno Indians. Not so much people in Fresno. But in other towns. Modesto."

"How appropriate in your case."

She daintily set her smoke down, turned around and poked me in the ribs hard, forcing me back into focus. She was wild-eyed. "Don't fucking say 'poor Armenians!' You're disrespecting my parents."

She was not really angry although she had me fooled for a moment. She ran her fingers down my bones like a harpist and we slept the sleep of the whacked until drizzly dawn. Getting up, it struck me that I was due in New York in less than a week and what fun Lucy was. She would be on location in Mendocino until I left. This saddened our morning. We swore to keep in touch, the contemporary West Coast vow of enduring passion.

The gig in New York was the rewrite of a script that had been worked by two different writers unaware of each other's efforts. The dawning era of serious adult movies (a term which did not then altogether carry the meaning it has today) had inspired them both to attempts at revolutionizing the film idiom. They both seemed to think that some ideal director would be guided by their novel scene settings and subtle dialogue. The thing had to be done in New York because the indispensable star lived in Bucks County and hated the coast. Naturally the synthesis was a turgid rat's nest and the job shameful and distressing. It was a project only God could have saved; I failed. I didn't like failing but I got paid and thanks to Him the thing never got made. If it had you can be sure I would have eaten the rap for it all by myself.

Then a doctoring job on a picture in production in England came my way. The project was an Englishing of a French movie for which the producers had actually paid money, and the translation of it by a British writer in command of good French was not at all bad. But the setting had been transferred to Queens, and the producers thought his draft both too faithful to the original and too un-American. This was one to grab though, a worthwhile credit. I went over, got hired, and started looking for a pad. Meanwhile the producers put me up in a crummy room at Brown's. The weather was sleety so I read my way through Olivia Manning's trilogies, Balkan and Levant. At this time Britain had no daytime television lest weak-minded people play hooky from their dark satanic mills. For the same reason nighttime television went off around eleven, to the national anthem.

One night I turned on the tube to see that ITV was running a soap Lucy had done two years before. The moment I recognized her I felt a rush, a fond longing. I wasn't inclined to explore the feeling. Without prejudice—I think without prejudice—I was struck with how good she was in it. She looked altogether youthful and lovely and she had a substance in the role that was worlds away from the poor

Pocahontas routine my pal John had thrust on her. Days later I watched another episode. She played a villainous character—slim sexy brunettes were usually villainesses then—who did a lot of lying. She managed to render deceit without sideward glances or eyerolling. Her character had heart and mystery. Also intelligence. Vanished were the trace elements of Valley Girl adolescence that I had become rather fond of. But I preferred Lucy the pro because in those days I loved watching real artists deliver.

Now I wonder if it wasn't about then—that early in the game— that I started doubting myself, distrusting the quality of the silence in which I worked. Anyway, in Lucy's performance on that soap I thought I recognized the effort of one who lived for doing the voices, the way good writers did. Equipped with a sheath of fictional identity, she turned incandescent.

In the morning I phoned her across eight time zones and tried to tell her what I had seen her do. She tried to tell me how she'd done it. Neither of us in that sudden conversation quite succeeded.

So I asked her: "How's life?"

She said: "Oh man, don't ask me. I don't know, you know? Sometimes bearable. At others fucked."

"The pains of love or what?"

"I miss you," she said all at once and I told her, from the heart, that I missed her too. I hadn't been asking her about us but I can tell you she put me in the moment.

The next day I got a call from John, the perpetrator of *Unbound Unleashed Uncooked*. During our conversation I had mentioned to Lucy that I was house hunting. John told me that none other than Heathcliff, Brion Pritchard, had an apartment in St. John's Wood I could borrow for a moderate fee. I was so enthused, and tired of hearing landlords either hang up or purr with greed at the sound of an American voice, that I went for it at once. The studio that had greenlighted us paid. Distracted, I failed to focus on the distastefulness of this arrangement. Anyway, prowling and prying about the place when

I should have been writing I discovered many amusing and scandalous things about Mr. and Mrs. Heathcliff that sort of endeared them to me.

Then a strange and wonderful thing happened. One evening at the interval of a play at the Royal Court I saw a girl—and she was so lovely and gamine that I could not think of that creature as anything but a girl—who was speaking American English to a female friend she had come with. I noticed that she was wearing Capezios. Catching her alone for a moment I made my move. My predations back in the day often had a theatrical background.

"You're a dancer," I told her.

She was in fact a dancer. I asked her if she cared for dinner or coffee or a drink after the play, but she didn't want to leave her friend alone. Today I would have given her my phone number, but not then, so I asked for hers and she gave it to me. On our first date we went to an Italian place in Hampstead. Jennifer had spent two years with the Frankfurt Ballet and when we met she was in England pondering options. European cities were losing their state art subsidies and there was no shortage of young dancers from Britain and the States. I took her home, not pressing it. Our second meeting was on Highgate Hill and as we walked to Ken Wood we told each other the story of our lives. This was the wonder-of-me stage of our courtship and it was genuinely sweet.

It turned out that Jennifer, notwithstanding her adorable long-toothed smile and freckled nose, had been around the block, a runaway child and an exotic dancer—a teenage stripper—in New Orleans. Her nice parents in River Oaks had reclaimed her and sent her back to ballet school, first in Dallas, finally in New York. As a student she had gotten into cocaine and danced a *Nutcracker* in Princeton where the falling snow effects, she said, made her sneeze. We were so easy with each other, at the same time so intoxicated. It was lovely.

In London, although there was plenty of blow about, she abstained and in that hard-drinking city she stayed sober. She put up with my boozing, but sweetly let me know she did not want to see the other. I thought often about moving her into the place on Abbey Road. Since the Pritchards showed no sign of returning I had stayed in it after the script was done and kept it on my own for months afterward, working on originals. For some reason we never quite got to the point of moving in together that year. Then I got a call—like all your Hollywood Calling calls it came in the middle of the night— asking me if I would come out and talk about another deathless number. I decided to go and when I told Jennifer she cried.

"I thought we were long-term."

It just about broke my heart. "We are long-term," I hastened to say. I wondered if she would ask to come with me. I probably would have taken her. At the same time I wanted to see Lucy.

Back in L.A. it was dry, sunny winter inland with a mellow marine layer at the beach each morning. The place I liked that I could have was a condo in Laguna. Laguna was pretty nice then but for some reason I had not known about the traffic and had not quite realized what was happening to Orange County. The apartment overlooked the sea and had sunsets.

I had batted out three original scripts in London. Mysteriously, the first two drew from my then agent—Mike? Marty?—more apparent sympathy than admiration. Out in the movie world two of them were promptly skunked. I was still used to being the boy wonder and a midlife bout of rejection was unappealing. I didn't much like rejection. Maybe I had tried too hard, attempting to scale the new peaks of serious and adult, naïvely imagining for myself an autonomy that neither I nor anyone in the industry possessed. The third one anyway was optioned, went into turnaround and years later actually got made. But my deathless number expired.

Frustrated and depressed I postponed calling Lucy. During my third week back I finally invited her down for another walk on the beach.

Climbing out of her dusty Jag she looked nothing but fine. She wore turquoise and a deerskin jacket, my Fresno Indian. With her smooth tan, her skin was the color of coffee ice cream and her eyes were bright. Ever since watching her perform in the soap I had begun to think of her as beautiful.

As we set out down the beach, beside the Pacific again, she put on a baseball cap that said Hussong's Cantina, promoting the joint in Ensenada. It was a sunny day even at the shore and you might have called the sea sparkling. A pod of dolphins patrolled outside the point break, gliding on air, making everything in life look easy. Lucy told me she had tested for a part in our friend John's next movie, a horror picture. She was still worried about whether he had somehow spotted the two of us walking out of Grauman's. The horror flick sounded like another bomb at best. This time Lucy had read the shooting script and knew what there was to know of the plot.

"She's a best friend. Supposed to be cute and funny. She dies."

I said that in my opinion she, Lucy, was ready for comedy.

"Tom, everyone pretty much dies horribly except the leads. It's a horror flick."

We had a nice day and night.

A week later I went up to Silver Lake where Lucy had moved after selling her nice trailer in Malibu. Her bungalow had some plants out front with an orangey spotlight playing on them, and in its beam I saw that the glass panels on her front door were smashed and the shards scattered across her doorway. Among them were pieces of what looked like a dun-colored Mexican pot. This was all alarming since her door would now admit all that lived, crawled, and trawled in greater L.A. Moreover, there was blood. When she let me in I asked her about it but got no answer. She brought us drinks and I lit a joint I had brought and she began to cry. Suddenly she gave me a sly smile that in the half-darkness of the patio reminded me of the weeping Indian maid I had rescued on the next seat at Grauman's.

"I'm in difficulty," she said.

I said I could see that. It turned out to be all about bloody Heathcliff, Brion Pritchard, still on the scene and newly cast in the horror movie. Third-rate art was staggering toward real life again;

Brion was the man who got to stab her repeatedly in the forthcoming vehicle.

"How can they do that?" I asked her. "Another of John's movies and Pritchard gets to kill you again. Isn't that like stupid?"

"He's relentless," she said. "Tommy, don't ask! What do I know?"

I suppose it was I who should have known. Brion was in serious decline, succumbing to occupational ailments in a tradition that went back to the time of nickelodeons. He drank. A man of robust appetites, he also smoked and snorted and stuffed and swallowed. On top it all he had started lifting weights and pioneering steroids. He boozed all day and through the night, drove drunk, punched some of the wrong people. Along the Rialto, all this was being noted and remarked upon. He was a violent working-class guy, one of A. E. Housman's beautiful doomed ploughboys, who but for talent and fortune would have drunk himself into Penrhyndeudraeth churchyard long before. Predictably, he had identified Lucy as the font of his troubles.

Shortly after dawn on the morning before my visit Brion had come banging on Lucy's door, haranguing her in elegant English and low Welsh. Impatient to enter and mess with her, he had taken her ornamental pot and shoved in the door, cutting himself in the process, badly enough to sober him slightly and slow him down. This bought time for Lucy to call 911. She told me that when the cops came Brion gave them the old Royal Shakespeare, which by then in Hollywoodland impressed no one. They all but begged her to press charges although he had only succeeded in hitting her once, hard. Naturally she denied it heroically—I could well picture her playing that one—and sent them away. At least she hadn't raced to his side at the hospital.

That evening it was plain we were not going to have much of a party. I asked Lucy to come down to Laguna with me. She dawdled and I hung around until she tuned me out. I was angry; moreover I was feeling too much like what you might call a confidante. In the end I made her swear to get the door fixed, even replaced, and I said

I'd do it if she wouldn't. I told her to call the cops and me if the loutish Welshman accosted her again. I have to admit that if it came to action I wanted the cops on my side.

Driving back that night was depressing. I had expected to stay with her. I should mention that in this period there occurred the last brief gas panic—odd and even numbered days and so on. In my opinion the fuel shortages of those years played their part in the vagaries of romance. People often went to bed with each other because their tanks were low.

I picked up work at that point with HBO, which had then started showing its own productions. The project involved some interviews around the country in the subjects' hometowns. It was a Vietnam War story, echoing the anger of the recent past. This took me out of town for the next three weeks. In a hotel in Minneapolis I picked up a *USA Today* with a back-page story announcing that Brion Pritchard was dead. It was shocking, though in fact with the advent of AIDS a sense of mortality increasingly pervaded. We could not know it but death was coming big time. In that innocent age no one had imagined that anything more serious would happen to Brion than his dropping a barbell on his foot. I felt nothing at first, no relief, no regret. He was no friend of mine. On the way back to L.A. though, I became drunk and depressed, as if a fellow circus performer had fallen from a high wire. All of us worked without a net.

I had some doubts about calling Lucy too soon, mainly because I no longer fancied the role of consoler. Eventually I realized that if I wanted to see her again I would have to endure it. When I called she sounded more confused than stricken. At first I couldn't be sure I had the right person on the line. My thought was: she doesn't know how she feels. This is a role thrust on her and her feelings are down in some dark inaccessible region much overlaid. With what? Childish hungers, history, drama school? Capped by unacknowledged work and guilty ambition. A little undeserved notoriety of the tabloid sort. By then I thought I knew a few things about actors. I had even been one years before.

When I saw Lucy next she gave a display of what I now recognized as false cheer. In this dangerous state she could appear downright joyous. When I expressed sympathy over Brion she gave me an utterly blank look. Being the pro she was, Lucy was almost always aware of how she looked but the expression she showed me was unpremeditated, unintentionally conveying to me that Pritchard's death was literally none of my business, that neither I nor anyone else shared enough common ground with her and the late Heathcliff, *ensemble*, for even polite condolences. But, somehow, a couple of weeks later we found ourselves on the road to Enseneda. Enseneda and Tijuana could still be raggedy fun in those days. We managed to borrow a warped convertible from an actor pal and took off down the coast road. I hope we told him we were crossing the border.

The drive was an idyll, precisely defined, I was unsurprised to learn, as a happy episode, typically an idealized or unsustainable one. Down south that April afternoon there were still a few blossoming orange groves to mix memory and desire on the ocean breeze. Over the emerald cliffs people were hang gliding, boys and alpha girls swooping like buzzards on the updrafts. In the sea below surfers were bobbing, pawing ahead of the rollers to catch the curl. And on the right, a gorgeous gilt—no golden—dome displayed a sign that read, as I recall: SELF-REALIZATION GOLDEN WORLD FELLOWSHIP. It was the place the surfer kids called Yogi Beach and there we overcame Lucy's peculiar grief and spent the happiest half-day of our lives.

In Tijuana, which was as far as we got, we put the convertible in Caesar's protected parking and ate the good steak and the famous salad. We did not talk about Brion. For a while we traded recollections of Brooklyn College drama school where, strangely, both of us had put in time.

It seemed, as the day lengthened, that the elations of our trip stirred a mutual yearning. Not about the night because of course the night would be ours. I thought we might find our way through the dazzle of our confusions to something beyond. In my memory of that day—or in my fond dream of a memory—I was about to guide us there. In this waking dream I'm suspended at the edge of a gesture or the right words. All at once a glimmer of caution flickers, goes out, flashes again. Who was she after all? An actor, above all. I was wary of how she brought out the performer in me. I mean the performer at the core, ready to follow her out on the wire where she lived her life. At that age I thought I might walk it too.

I could have been a moment short of giving her the sign she wanted, whatever it was. These days I sometimes imagine that with the right words, a touch, a look, I might have snatched her out of disaster's path, away from the oncoming life that was gathering ahead of her. I held back. Surely that was wise. The moment passed and then Lucy simply got distracted.

I let us drift down the collonnades of the farmacia tour at the busy end of Revolución, chasing green crosses and phosphorescence. I wanted a party too. Joy's hand, they say, is always at his lips bidding adieu. That melancholy truth drove us.

We crossed back to Yanquilandia without incident. On the drive up the freeways we talked about ourselves.

"You and me," Lucy asked. "What is *that?*"

I didn't know. I said it was a good thing.

"Where would it go?"

Not into the sunset, I thought. I said exactly that. Lucy was ripped. She chattered.

"Everything goes there," she told me.

I ought not to have been driving. I was stoned myself.

As Lucy talked on I kept changing the subject or at least tweaking it.

"I have a kind of plan for my life," she said. "Part of it is career shit." She had picked up the contemporary habit of referring to people's film and stage work that way, including her own. As in "I want to get my shit up there." Or "I saw you in whatever it was and I loved your shit." It was thought to be unpretentious and hip, one social deviant to another. I particularly hated it, perhaps for pertinent but at the time unconscious reasons. "Actually," she went on with an embarrassed laugh, "artistic ambitions."

"Why not?"

Her fancies involved going east to Off-Broadway. Or working in Europe. Or doing something in one of the independent productions that were beginning to find distribution. Beside the artistic ambitions she entertained some secular schemes for earning lots of money in pictures. In retrospect, these were unrealistic. We found ourselves back on the subject of us.

"Don't you love me?" she asked.

"You know I do."

"I hope so. You're the only one who ever knew I was real."

I politely denied that but I thought about it frequently thereafter.

"What about Brion?"

"Poor Brion was a phantom himself," she said.

"Really? He threw a pretty solid punch for a phantom."

"I wasn't there that time either," she said. "I hardly felt it."

Passing the refinery lights of Long Beach she shook her head as though she were trying to clear it of whispers.

"You know," she said, "as far as shadows and ghosts go, I fear my own."

"I understand," I said. Hearing her say it chilled me but for some reason I *did* understand, thoroughly. I was coming to know her as well as was possible.

"Why do you always treat me with tea-party manners, Tom?"

"I don't. I don't even know what you mean."

"You're always trying to be funny."

I said that didn't mean I didn't love her. "It's all I know," I said.

We were driving along the margins of a tank farm that stood beside the freeway. Its barbed chain-link fence was lined with harsh prison yard arc lights that lit our car interior as we passed and framed us in successive bursts of white glare. In my delusion, the light put me in mind of overbright motel corridors with stained walls tunneling through some gnomish darkness. My head hurt. In the spattered white flashes I caught her watching me. I thought I could see the reflected arc lights in her eyes and the enlarged pupils almost covering their irises, black on black.

"Everybody loves you, Tom," she said. "Don't they?"

How sad and lonely that made me feel. Out of selfishness and need I actually grieved for myself. It passed.

"Yes, I'm sure everyone does. It's great."

"Do I count?" she asked.

Yes and no. But of course I didn't say that. In the twisted light I saw her out there sauntering toward a brass horizon and I wanted to follow after. But I was not so foolish nor had I the generosity of spirit. I was running out of heart.

"You more than anyone, Lucy," I said. "Only you really."

That's how I remember it. As we drove on Lucy began to complain about a letter she said I'd written.

"You used these exquisite phrases. Avoiding the nitty-gritty. All fancy dancing."

"I don't do that. I don't know what letter you mean. Come on— 'exquisite phrases'?" I laughed at her.

A couple of miles later she informed me she had written the letter to herself. "In my style," she said.

"So," I asked her, "what were the phrases you liked?"

"I don't remember. I wanted to get it down. The way you are."

"Lucy, please don't write letters from me to yourself. I can do it."

"You never wrote me," she said, which I guess was partly the point. "Anyone can jump out of a phone."

Suddenly though, without apparent spite she declared: "John's going to expand my part." She was talking about the now-revived horror movie in which John had hired a live British actor to strangle her. However, on consideration she thought he might now transform her into a surviving heroine. I said it was great but that it probably wouldn't be as much fun.

"You know," she said, "you don't get credit for being scared and dying. It doesn't count as acting. Anyway I can live without fun."

"If you say so."

"John," she said, "wants to marry me." For some reason at that point she put her hand on my knee and turned her face to me. "Seriously."

I wondered about that for a while in the weeks following. Once she showed me a postcard of the Empire State Building he had sent her from New York. He had adorned it with embarrassing jokey scribbles about his erection. One day I took John to Musso's for lunch but he said not a word to me about her. Over our pasta I asked him if it was true that he was sparing Lucy's character in the thing forthcoming.

"Oh," he said, as though it was something that had slipped his mind. "Absolutely. Lucy's time has come."

I suspected that the lead would be the kind of supposed-to-be-feisty female lately appearing as part of the serious and adult wave. I knew Lucy could deliver that one all the way from Avenida Revolución.

"She can give a character some inner aspects," I told him.

"You're so right."

"Good actress," I suggested. "Great kid."

John went radiant but he didn't look like a bridegroom to me. "You know it, Tom. Tops."

He didn't marry Lucy. Instead, when the funeral-baked meats had cooled he married Brion Pritchard's widow, Maerwyn. He didn't even promote Lucy to insipid ingénue. Halfway through the horror movie her character died like a trooper. In spite of my infatuation I had to admit there were many great things one could do with Lucy but marrying her was probably not one of them.

We went out a few times. She began to seem to me—for lack of a better word—unreal. I kept trying to get close to her again. At the time I was selling neither scripts nor story ideas. There were no calls. I might have tried for an acting gig; I was owed a few favors. I had no illusions about my talent but I was cheap and willing, well-spoken enough for walk-ons as a mad monk or war-mongering general. I offered a Brooklyn Heights accent, which sounds not at all the way you think. But I had grown self-conscious and all the yoga in the world wasn't going to bring back my chops or my youthful arrogance. That was what I'd need in front of a camera. My main drawback as an actor had always been a tendency to perform from the neck up. I might have thrived in the great days of radio.

Somehow I got a job with a newspaper chain working as their West Coast editor. It took up a lot of my time and part of my work was resisting being transformed into a gossip columnist. I almost got fired for doing a piece for the *New York Times* Arts and Leisure section. The news chain paid a lot less than writing for the movies but it paid regularly. I had plans to engineer a spread for Lucy but nothing came along to hang it on.

Out of what seemed like nowhere she took up with a friend of mine named Asa Maclure, pronounced *Mac*-lure, whom people called Ace. Ace was an actor and occasional writer (mostly of blaxploitation flix during the seventies) with whom I had liked to go out drinking and drugging and what we insensitively called wenching. Ace was a wild man. What inclined me to forgive him at all was a telegram he had once sent to a director in Washington for whom he was going to act Othello.

CANT WAIT TO GET MY HANDS AROUND THAT WHITE WOMAN'S THROAT.

Ace had just arrived back in L.A. from Africa where he had portrayed a loyal askari who saved a blonde white child from swart Moorish bandits in the Sahara. The white child, supposed to be French, was from Eastern Europe somewhere. Ace was unclear as to which country. She had gone on location with her mother along as chaperone. The mom was, as Ace put it, a babe. Ace was suave and beautiful, the kind of guy they would cast as Othello. In no time at all his romance, as they say, with Mrs. Vraniuk was the talk of every location poker game. Restless under the desert sky Ace decided to shift his attention to young Miss Vraniuk. Consummation followed, producing some uneasiness since the kid was not yet twenty-one. Nor was she eighteen. Nor, it seemed, perhaps, was she fifteen. But it was in another country, another century, a different world. At the time, in the circumstances, it represented no more than a merry tale.

"This child was ageless, man," Ace told us. "She had the wiles of Eve."

If any images or other evidence of desert passion existed, no one worried much about it. Talk was cheap. And most American tabloids then did not even buy pictures.

Ace and Lucy became a prominent item, appearing in the very magazine that now employed me. The stories were fueled by Ace's sudden trajectory toward stardom. Though she was blooming, as she aged more beautiful then ever, she was noticed only as Ace's companion.

It happened that one week the papers dispatched me with a photographer to do a story on kids in South Central who rode high stakes bike races. The races ran on barrio streets, inviting the wagers of high rolling meth barons and senior gangbangers. Lucy decided to come with me and when I went down a second time she came along again. Both times she seemed a little hammered and could not be discouraged from flirting with a few speed-addled pistoleros. A local actually approached me with a warning that she was behaving unwisely. Driving back to Silver Lake she said: "You and I are sleepwalking."

"How do you mean?" I asked her.

"We're unconscious. Living parallel lives. We never see each other."

I said I thought she was involved with Ace.

"I mean really see each other, Tommy. The way people can see each other."

"You're the one who's sleepwalking, Lucy."

"Oh," she said, "don't say that about me." She sounded as though she had been caught out, trapped in something like a lie. "That's frightening."

"That's what you said about both of us. I thought you were on to something."

Maybe she was confounded at her own inconsistency. More likely she never got there. She sat silent for a while. Then she said: "Don't you understand. Tommy. It's always you with me. Ever since Grauman's."

It was not a joke. I don't think she meant to hurt or deceive me with the things she said. For some reason, though, she could leave me feeling abandoned and without hope. Not only about us but about everything. She was concerned with being there. And with whom to be. It occurred to me that perhaps she was going through life without, in a sense, knowing what she was doing. Or that she was not doing anything but forever being done. Waiting for a cue, a line, a vehicle, marks, blocking. Somewhere to stand and be whoever she might decide she was, even for a moment.

"That can't be true, Lucy."

"Oh yes," she said, urgently, deeply disturbed, "Oh yes baby, it is true."

There was no point in arguing. A couple of miles along, she put her hand on my driving arm, holding it hard and I suspected she might force the wheel.

"I have such strength," she said. "I don't know how to use it. Or when. I accommodate. That's the trouble."

One strange afternoon, Asa Maclure, Lucy, and myself decided to go bungee jumping. Seriously. It might have represented the zenith of our tattered glory days. The place we chose to bungee jump from was a mountainside high above the Mojave flats, reachable by cable car from Palm Springs. There, over a rock face that rose a sheer few hundred feet from the desert floor, two actual Australians, a boy and a girl, had the jump concession.

I might say that I can't imagine how we came to plan this but in fact I know how. Ace was well aware of the fraught status between Lucy and myself. I'm sure she talked about me to him, maybe a lot. He would tease me, or both of us, when we were together.

"You all are actually pathetic," he declared once. "A gruesome two-some. Tommy, she sighs and pines over you. I believe you do the same. I don't mind."

I was provoked. He was saying that our strange affair notwith-standing, he—Mister Mens Sana in Corpore Sano—was who she turned to for good loving. It was a taunt. So I decided I'd play some soul poker with him for Lucy and win and take her away. Thereafter he tried to see that she avoided me. When we were all together Ace and I would watch each other for cracks in which to place a wedge. Though I liked to believe I was smarter than Ace, he was verbally quite agile.

The bungee incident began as a bad joke and started overheating, the way one kid's playful punch of another will gradually lead to an angry fistfight. In fact it was completely childish, nothing less than a dare. It was I who made the mistake of talking bungee jump; I'd seen the Australians referred to in the *Times*'s weekend supplement and it occurred to me I might get my employers to pay for us. Ace was famous, Lucy semi-famous, beginning to get noticed, frequently called in to test, and cast at times to help lesser actors look good. There were also reruns of her several soaps.

I felt I had to do this. I had made a jocular reference to this scheme in the presence of Ace, and Lucy and Ace called me on it. While I was trying to prod the higher powers to spring and assign a photographer the two of them went and did it. Would Lucy descend into the pon-derosa-scented void after her paramour? A thing never in question. It was an eminence she'd sought lifelong, a Fuji disposable Lover's Leap. They survived.

All my life I have regretted not being there. For one thing, regard-ing *Mac*lure, I held my manhood cheap. He had foxed me and bonded with her in a way that I, who had made something of a career out of witnessing Lucy's beau gestes, would never experience. She hurt me bad.

Suffering is illuminating, as they say, and in my pain I almost learned something about myself. I repressed the insight. I was not ready, then, to yield to it.

"I wanted it to be you," Lucy said, like a deflowered prom queen apologizing to the high school athlete whose lettered jersey she had worn and dishonored.

"I wanted it to be me too," I said. "Why did you go and do it?"

"I was afraid I wouldn't do it if we waited."

I shouted at her, something I very rarely did.

"You'd have done it with me! You goddamn well would have!"

Of course this exchange was as juvenile as the rest of the incident but it stirred the unconsidered home truth I had been resisting. This kind of juvenalia goes deep and you can also approach self-awareness after acting childishly.

Still, I wasn't up to facing it. For days and days I went to sleep, stoned, half-drunk, whispering: What was it like, Lucy? I meant the leap. I very nearly went bungee jumping by myself but it seemed a sterile exercise.

I was bitter. I had excuses to avoid her and I used them all. She called me at the office and in Laguna but I was tired of it. The next thing I knew I had quit my job and gone over to England to find Jennifer.

Jen had got a Green Book and was teaching dance with some friends in Chester. When we saw each other I knew it was on again. I had to peel her loose from some painter from over the border. Another fucking Welsh boyfriend!

I took her home to Dallas and met the high-toned folks and married her in the high-toned Episcopal equivalent of a nuptial mass, dressed up like a character out of Oscar Wilde. She conscientiously wore red, though I pointed out that neither of us had been married before. We moved to Laguna and, lovely and smart as she was, Jen got herself a tenure-track job in dance at UC San Diego. I watched her work and she was peppy and the good cop bad cop kind of teacher, and you never saw a prettier backside in a leotard. We moved to Encinitas.

My bride all but supported me while I worked on a few scripts. She had loans from her parents and the UC salary. I don't know exactly what had changed in the movie business; I hadn't noticed anything good. However I optioned two scripts right away.

One day I was coming out of the HBO offices on Olympic when I ran into Asa Maclure. The sight of him froze my heart. In those years you knew what the way he looked meant. He was altogether too thin for his big frame, his cool drape sagged around him. The worst of it was his voice, always rich, Shakespearean, his preacher father's voice. It had become a rasp. He sounded old and he looked sad and wise, a demeanor that he had used to assume in jest. I hoped he wouldn't mention the bungee jump but he did. Plainly it meant a lot to him. From a different perspective, it did to me too. We traded a few marginally insincere laughs about how absurd the whole thing had been. He looked so doomed I couldn't begrudge him the high they must have had. I didn't ask him how he was.

A couple of weeks later I got a call from Lucy and she wanted to see me. She was still in Silver Lake. I lied to Jennifer when I drove up to visit her. Jen had not asked where I was going but I volunteered false information. I felt profoundly unfaithful though I realized that there was not much likelihood of my sleeping with Lucy. No possibility at all, from my point of view. So I felt unfaithful to her too.

Lucy, in Silver Lake, seemed at once agitated and exhausted.

"Ace said he saw you," she told me, when we were seated in the patio dead Heathcliff had demolished.

Passing through her living room I noticed that the house was in a squalid state. The floors were littered with a scatter of plastic flowers and charred metal cylinders. There were roaches on the floor and in the ashtrays, along with beer cans and other post-party knickknacks. Lucy had been running with a new set of friends. I imagined these people as a kind of simian troop, although I never got it clear who exactly they were and how Lucy had been impressed into being their hostess. I did know that it had somehow to do with supply and demand.

I had been out of town and I was not familiar with free-basing. I can't be sure that Asa turned her on to it. Basing was the rage then in extremist circles like his. She talked about it with a rapturous smile. I had been around long enough to remember when street drugs hit the industry big time, and I remembered that smile from the days when each new advance in narcosis had been acclaimed as somebody's personal Fourth of July. A life-changing event. To cool the rock's edges Lucy had taken to easing down behind a few upscale pharmaceuticals: 'ludes, opiate pills. Unfortunately for all of us, genuine quaaludes were disappearing even south of the border. This left the opiates, which were still dispensed with relative liberality. While I watched, Lucy cooked up the brew in her kitchen as she had been instructed. She told me she had always liked to cook though this was a side of her I'd never seen.

Cooking base, we ancients of art will recall, involved a number of tools. Seven-Elevens then sold single artificial flowers in test tube–like containers so that crack scenes were sometimes adorned with sad false blossoms. Lucy mixed quite a few gram baggies with baking soda and heated them in a cunning little Oriental pot. The devil of details was in the mix, which Lucy approached with brisk confidence. Alarmingly, the coke turned into viscous liquid. People who have put in time in really crappy motels may recall finding burned pieces of coat hanger on the floor of the closets or wardrobes. Lucy had one and she used it to fish the brew out so it could cool and congeal. It was then that the stem came into play and a plastic baby bottle and a burned wad of Chore Boy, which was a kind of scouring pad we used as a filter. On the business end of the stem, appropriately enough, was the bottle's nipple, which the adept lipped like a grouper on brain coral.

We did it and at first it reminded me of how, when I was a child, my mother would have me inhale pine needle oil to cure a chest cold. The effect however was different, although if someone had told me it cured colds I wouldn't have argued. It was quite blissful for a time and we were impelled toward animated chatter. I commenced to instruct Lucy on the joys of marriage, for which I was then an enthusiast. She soared with me; her eyes flashed. In this state she was always something to see.

"I'm so happy for you. No I'm really not. Yes I am."

We smoked for an hour or more. As she plied the hanger end to scrape residue from the filter and stem, she told me about her career prospects, which seemed stellar. She had been cast for what seemed a good part in a film by a notoriously eccentric but gifted director who had assembled a kind of repertory company for his pictures. Some of these made money, some tanked, but all of them got some respect. For Lucy, this job was a good thing. And not only was there the film part. As schedules permitted, she was going to do Irina in *Uncle Vanya* at a prestigious neighborhood playhouse. I rejoiced for her. As I was leaving, supremely confident and looking forward to the drive, I kissed her. Her response seemed less sensual than emotional. I was hurt, although I had no intention of suggesting anything beyond our embrace. Sometimes you just don't know what you want.

Around Westminster, I began to feel the dive. Its sensation was accompanied by a sudden suspicion that Lucy's reversal of fortune might be a little too good to be true. When I got home I took two of the pain pills and believed her again.

Not long after this we read that Asa Maclure was dead too. He had AIDS all right but it wasn't the disease that killed him. The proximate cause of his death was an accident occasioned by his unsteady attempt to cook some base. He set himself on fire, ran as fast as he could manage out of his San Vicente apartment and took off down the unpeopled sidewalks of the boulevard. He ran toward the ocean. Hundreds of cars passed him as he ran burning. According to some alleged witnesses even a fire truck went by, although that may have been someone's stroke of cruel wit.

Asa Maclure was a wonderful man. He was, as they say, a damn good actor. He was also enormous fun. In the end, he was a good friend too, although obviously a difficult one. Suffice it to say I mourned him.

Jennifer and I went to his funeral. It was held at a freshly painted but rickety-looking black church in what had once been a small southern town not thirty miles from where her parents lived in River Oaks. Asa's father presided, his master in declamation. Asa had resembled his father and the man was strong and prevailed over his grief. There were few people from the industry, mostly African-American, all male. Praise God, Lucy did not appear.

Back in Dallas at my in-laws' stately home we had a few bourbons.

"Your friend has the kiss of death," Jennifer said. She delivered this observation without inflection but it remained to hover on the magnolia-scented air of that cool, exquisitely tasteful room.

Both of my optioned scripts were being green-lighted.

From what I read in the papers it seemed Lucy had been replaced in the mad genius' picture. The neighborhood production of *Vanya* opened with no mention of her. I presumed she had read for it. Maybe she had assumed the part was hers. Once I met her for a sandwich in a Beverly Hills deli and we talked about Ace's death. Lucy spoke slowly, with great precision and was obviously high. I was worried about her and also concerned to discover where Ace's death had left her.

"I've compartmentalized my life," she declared. She had brought with her a huge paperback book with dog-eared pages and she showed it to me. It was a collection of drawings by Giovanni Piranesi that featured his series called "Imaginary Prisons," in which tiers of prison cells are ranked along Gothic stone staircases and upon the battlements of vast dungeons that ascend and descend over spaces that appear infinite. For reasons which many art lovers will immediately comprehend on seeing some of his drawings, Piranesi is a great favorite among cultivated junkies. His prisons are like their world.

On the blank pages in the book Lucy had written what she called plans. These were listed in columns placed across from one another, each laid out in variously colored inks and displaying Lucy's runic but attractive handwriting. When she handed the book to me for comment I could only utter a few appreciative sounds. Every word in every paragraph of every column was unreadable. I still have no idea what she had written there. Finally I could not, for my life, keep myself from saying something meant to be friendly and comforting about Asa. I got the same cold suffering look I had seen when Brion Pritchard died.

In the weeks after that, in a craven fashion, I kept my distance from her because I was afraid of what I might see and hear. She didn't call. Also the trip to Texas had left Jen and me closer somehow—at least for a while.

After a few months Lucy left a message on our machine absurdly pretending to be someone else. Suddenly I thought I wanted to see her again. The desire, the impulse, came over me all at once in the middle of a working afternoon. On re-examination, I think the urge was partly romantic, partly Pavlovian. I was concerned. I wanted to help her. I wanted to get seriously high with her because Jen didn't use. So my trip back to Silver Lake was speeded by a blend of high-mindedness and base self-indulgence. It's a fallen world, is it not? We carry love in earthen vessels.

Lucy's house was not as dirty and disorderly as it had been on my last visit but everything still looked dingy. She did not garden or wash windows and no longer employed her help. She no longer cooked either since crack, the industrialized version of base, had obviated that necessity. It was safer too and far less messy than basing. The rocks went straight from the baggie into the stem. For me the hit was even better. She had Percocet and Xanax for coming down, a lot of it. She was still very attractive and I later learned she had a thing going with a druggy doc in Beverly Hills who must have been something of an adventurer.

"I'm going to Jerusalem!" she said. She said it so joyously that for a second I thought she had got herself saved by some goof.

"Yes?" I approved wholeheartedly. Seconds after the pipe I approved of nearly everything that way. "How great!"

"Listen to this!" she said. "I'm going there to live in the Armenian quarter. In a monastery. Or, like, a convent."

"Terrific! As a nun?"

She laughed and I did too. We laughed loud and long. When we were finished laughing she slapped me on the shoulder.

"No, ridiculous one! As research. Because I'm going to do a script about the massacres. I'm going to sneak into Anatolia and see the Euphrates."

She had an uncle who was a high-ranking priest at the see of the Jerusalem patriarch. He would arrange for her stay and she could interview survivors of the slaughter.

"I want to do this for my parents. For my background. I won't say 'heritage' because that's so pretentious."

"I think it's a great idea."

I was about, in my boisterous good humor, to call her project a pipedream. Fortunately I thought better of it.

She saw the thing as eminently possible. The Russians had unraveled and she might film in Armenia. There were prominent Armenian-Americans in the movie business, in town and in the former USSR. She had me about a quarter convinced though I wondered about the writing. She had the answer to that.

"This is yours, Tommy! Will you do it? Will you go with me? Will you think about it? Please? Because if you wrote it I'm sure I could direct. Because you know how it is. You and me."

Naturally the urgency was intense. "It's a sweet idea," I said.

"You could bring your wife, you know. I forget her name."

I told her. She had somehow deduced that Jennifer was younger than she.

"They're all named Jennifer," she said.

As if to bind me to the plan she pressed huge handfuls of Percocet on me. Starting to drive home I realized that I was too rattled to make it all the way to Encinitas. I checked into a motel that was an island of downscale on the Westwood-Santa Monica border and called Jen, home from her classes. I explained how I had come up to inquire into something or other, and suddenly felt too ill to make it back that evening.

"Don't drive then," Jen said. I could see trouble shimmering on the blacktop ahead.

Next Lucy disappeared. Her phone was suddenly out of service. The next time I was up in town I went to her house and found it unoccupied. The front garden was ochre rubble and the house itself enclosed in scaffolding. It was lunchtime and a work crew of Meso-Americans in faded flannel shirts were eating In-and-Out burgers on the roof.

Once I got a message in which she claimed to be in New York. It was rambling and unsound. She said some indiscreetly affectionate things but neglected to leave a number or address. I did my best to tape over the message to stay out of trouble. I had only partial success.

A little serendipity followed. I heard from a friend back in New York, a documentary filmmaker whom I hadn't seen in many years. He had gone into some boutique on Madison and met the gorgeous salesperson. She seemed glamorous and mysterious and dressed enticingly from the store so he asked her out. He thought she might go for a Stoppard play so he took her to the play and to Da Torcella and then to Nell's. People recognized her. It turned out she was an actor, a smart actor, and could talk Stoppard with insight. She was a wild but inspired dancer and had very nearly nailed a part in an actual Broadway play. She knew me, was in fact a friend of mine.

"Oh," I said. "Lucy."

He was disappointed she hadn't asked him home that night. Casual couplings were not completely out of fashion by then, though white balloons were beginning to ascend over West Eleventh Street. My friend thought he liked her very much but when he'd called one evening she sounded strange. It sounded, too, as though she lived in a hotel.

I thought I knew the story and I was right. She could hardly have asked him home because home then was an SRO on 123rd and Broadway and he would not have enjoyed the milieu. All her salary and commissions, as I later learned, were going for crack and for scag to mellow it out. Pain pills were not doing it any longer. I quoted him the maxim made famous by Nelson Algren: "Never go to bed with someone who has more problems than you do." He understood. I didn't think I had deprived anyone of their bliss.

There was something more to my friendly cautioning. It wasn't exactly jealousy. It was that somehow I thought I was the only one who could handle Lucy. That she was my parish.

When she showed up in California again it was in San Francisco. I got a call from her up there and this time I didn't bother to erase it. Jennifer and I were in trouble. I had a bit of a drug problem. I was drinking a lot. I suspected her of having an affair with some washed-up Bosnian ballet dancer she had hired down at UCSD. The fellow was supposed to be gay but I was suspicious. Jennifer was a well-bred, well-spoken East Texas hardass a couple of generations past share-cropping. Amazingly, the more I drank and used, the more she lost respect for me. At the same time I was selling scripts like crazy, rewriting them, sometimes going out on locations to work them through. Jennifer was largely unimpressed. Everything was stressful.

I was full of anger and junkie righteousness and I went up to see Lucy, hardly bothering to cover my tracks. She had rented an apartment there that belonged to her stockbroker sister, not a bad one at all though it was in the dreary Haight. I guess I had wanted a look at who Lucy's latest friends were.

Her live-in friend was Scott and she introduced us. I had expected a repellent creep. Scott surpassed my grisliest expectations. He had watery eyes, of a blue so pale that his irises seemed at the point of turning white. He had very thin trembly red lips that crawled up his teeth at one corner to form a kind of tentative sneer. He had what my mother would have called a weak chin, which she believed was characteristic of non-Anglo Saxons. There were no other features I recall.

Scott was under the impression he played the guitar. He plinked on one for us as we watched and waited. Lucy avoided eye contact with me. As Scott played his face assumed a kind of fanatical spirituality and he rolled his strange eyes. Watching him do it induced in the beholder something like motion sickness. In his transport he suggested the kind of Jehovah's Witness who would kill you with a hammer for rejecting his *Watchtower*.

When he had finished Lucy exclaimed: "Oh wow." By force of will I prevented us from applauding.

Scott's poison was methamphetamine. I was not yet familiar with the drug's attraction and this youth served as an exemplar. Having shot some, his expression shifted from visionary to scornful, paranoid and back. I had seen many druggy people over the years—I knew I was one myself—but Scott was a caution to cats. To compare his state with a mad Witness missionary was demeaning to believers. His transcendent expression, his transport, ecstasy, whatever, was centered on neurological sensation like a laboratory rat's. The mandala at the core of his universe was his own asshole. It was outrageous. However there we were, beautiful Lucy, cultivated me, livers of the examined life, in more or less the same maze. What did it make us?

When Scott had exhausted conversation by confusing himself beyond explication, he took a pair of sunglasses off the floor beside him, put them on and moved them up on his forehead.

"I invented this," he told us, "this pushing shades up on your head thing."

Weeks later Scott was removed from her apartment with the aid of many police officers, screaming about insects and imitating one. It was history repeating itself as farce, a particularly unfunny one. Lucy lost the place and the stockbroker sister was forced out. The upside was losing Scott as well.

Back home it was cold and Jennifer grew suspicious and discontent. When she was very angry her mild educated Anglo-Southern tones could tighten and faintly echo the speech of her remote sharecropping ancestors in the Dust Bowl. Sometimes her vowels would twist themselves into the sorrowful whine of pious stump farmers abandoned by Jesus in the bottomland. You had to listen very closely to hear it. I had never heard the word "honey" sound so leaden until Jennifer smacked me in the mouth with it. She could do the same thing with "dear." Dust Bowl, I thought was by then a useful summary of our married state.

I started going to bars. I listened to production assistants' stories about the new-style dating services. I did not pursue these routes because I was no longer so young and beautiful and because I was bitter and depressed. I did have a few one- or two-nighters on location. The best, carnally speaking, was with a stunt woman with a body like a Mexican comic book heroine who, it was said, had once beat an Arizona policeman half to death. Of course bodies like hers were not rare in movieland. Straight stunt girls were more fun, at least for me, than actresses. What they might lack in psychological dimension they made up for in contoured heft and feel and originality. They were sometimes otherwise limited unless you counted insanity as psychological dimension. Once I had a weeklong liaison with an unhappily married Las Vegas mounted policewoman who wanted to break into movies. As for the young women once characterized as starlets—they all knew the joke about the Polish ingénue, the one who slept with the writer.

I was not so obtuse that I failed to observe certain patterns in my own behavior—not simply the greedy self-indulgence but all the actions that were coming to define me. This seemed at the time a misfortune because I didn't reflect on them with any satisfaction. There they were however, beginning to seem like a summary, coming up like old bar bills. As for root causes, I couldn't have cared less. There were limits even to my self-absorption. Also I worried about getting ever deeper into drugs.

I saw Lucy every few months. Jennifer and I finally had it out around that one. She accused me of infidelity and I told her plainly that yes I was sleeping around. Safe sex of course, I said, though I don't know how much that would have mattered since we had not made love for months. However, I told her truthfully that I had not been to bed with Lucy for years and not at all since we had married. I also challenged her own virtue.

"What about your supposed-to-be-faggot colleague down there at school. Fucking Boris." The high-bouncing lover was called Ivan Ivanic and I had hated him since the day Jennifer corrected my pronunciation of his name, which was I-van-ich. "He's not getting in your pants?"

She was furious, naturally. You can't use that kind of malicious language about gays to most dancers. But I saw something else in her reaction. She was shocked. She cried. I resisted the impulse to believe her.

I visited Lucy more frequently. One thing I went up for was dope. She had moved into a fairly respectable hotel just uphill from the Tenderloin and by then she was scoring regularly in the Mission. After numerous misadventures, ripoffs, and a near rape she had learned how to comport herself around the market. She had the added protection of being a reliable customer. Lucy was not yet penniless. Her television work was still in syndication and her residuals from SAG continued. But she was spending her money fast.

By the time I arrived from the airport—this was still in the days of fifty-dollar flights—Lucy would have done her marketing on Dolores and picked up her exchange spike at the Haight Free Clinic. My contribution to the picnic was the coke I had bought down south. Lucy kept her small room very neat. We would embrace. Sometimes we would hold each other, as chaste as Hansel and Gretel, to show we cared. We hoped we cared. Both of us were beginning to stop caring about much.

I would snort coke and Lucy's smack. I never shot it.

Sometimes it made me sick. Often it provoked brief hilarity. I would watch her fix—the spoon, the lighter, the works as they say— with something like reverence. Listen, I had grown up to Chet Baker, to Coltrane, to Lady Day. To me, junkies, no matter how forlorn, were holy. Of course at a certain point if you've see one you've seen them all and this was as true of us as of anyone. Much of the time we looked into each other's eyes without sentiment. This was better than staring at your toe. In each other's dilating pupils we could reflect calmly on the uneasy past. The lambent moments expanded infinitely, all was resolved for a while. Once she even began to dream aloud about going to Jerusalem to do research for the script that I would write, and about kicking the jones in the Holy Places.

We chose silence sometimes. It wasn't that we never spoke. In a certain way you might say we were weary of each other. Not bored, or fed up, or anything of that sort. Worn out after the lives we'd tried to make intersect, and conducting a joint meditation on the subject. There were times I'll admit I cried. She never did but then she was always higher.

Every little once in a while Lucy would try to persuade me to fix the way she did. We never went through with it and I felt guilty. I was after all the guy who had not gone bungee jumping. Lucy never pressed it.

"If you died I would feel like I killed Shakespeare," she said.

I was never sure whether we thought this would be good or bad.

Mortality intruded itself regularly into our afternoons because it seemed that half the people we knew were dead. I supposed that down in sunny Encinitas my Jennifer was expecting to hear that I had succumbed to the kiss. During one of my later visits—one of the last—Lucy told me about a conversation she'd had at the UC hospital emergency room. A doctor there had said to her: "You're rather old to be an addict." She laughed about it and did a self-important, falsely mellow doctorish voice repeating it.

To me Lucy was still beautiful. I don't know how she looked to other people. She was my heroine. I noticed though that lately she always wore long sleeves and that it was to hide the abscesses that marked the tracks where her veins had been. Her eyes didn't die. Once she looked out the small clear window that looked up Nob Hill and made a declaration.

"The rest of my life is going to last about eleven minutes."

The line was hardly lyrical but her delivery was smashing. She looked great saying it and I saw that at long last she had located the role of her lifetime. Everything before had been provisional but she had made this woman her own. It was as though this was finally whom she had become and she could do almost anything with it. Found her moment, to be inhabited completely, but of course briefly.

I went home then, the way I always had, and saved almost everything. I saw that Lucy and I, together, had finally found the true path and that this time we were walking hand and hand, the whole distance. Again I refused the jump. She was more than half a ghost by then and it would be pretty to think her interceding spirit saved me.

One of us had to walk away and it was not going to be Lucy. She was the actor, I thought, not me.

The psychaitrist's
name was Paul, if
it   matters.
(Bukowski, page 63)

I Was in Flowers

Jonathan Ames

ABOUT FIVE YEARS AGO, I WENT TO SEE THIS MALE PROSTITUTE. I'm not gay, but something is wrong with me. Something happened in childhood.

So I saw this guy's ad in the *Village Voice* and called him. All it showed was his muscular torso. But that didn't really matter. I don't care what a man looks like. "I saw your ad," I said on the phone. The rest was pretty easy—price, address, time. He could see me in an hour. If it had been any longer, I probably wouldn't have gone. When you have a self-destructive compulsion you need to act on it fast.

He lived in a five-story walk-up on a busy avenue—bars, delis, restaurants, banks, and drug stores. He buzzed me through the vestibule. I climbed the dirty, anonymous stairs to the third floor and was so nervous I thought I might faint or have some kind of convulsion. I couldn't stop trembling. He opened the door a crack, saw I was harmless, and let me in.

He was wearing an old blue robe and had a glass of whiskey in his hand. He offered to make me a drink, but I only had a glass of water. He had me sit in this old-fashioned, men's-club armchair and he sat on his bed. It took small talk about the weather for me to stop shaking.

"What's it like out?" he said. "I haven't been out all day."

39

"It's a mild night," I said. It was early May, around eleven o'clock at night.

"I love spring," he said. "I need to get out."

His apartment was crowded and dark. The furniture was too big for a narrow studio. It was the kind of stuff that was supposed to look classy, like some middle-class family's notion of elegance in their living room (with a touch of hysteria or something)—an elaborate mirrored cabinet, gigantic stained-glass lamps, the armchair I was sitting in, and a faux-antique mobile-bar with lots of bottles. The wallpaper was a dark, boudoir-crimson.

The guy also added to the crowded feeling in the place. He was a big lug—about 6'4", 230 pounds, large masculine head, blunt American features, about forty-five, and his hair was close-cropped and receding. He looked like a dock worker, but his furniture was definitely a little queer.

He was a nice guy. Sweet. After he finished his whiskey, he gently asked me for the money and said that I should just put it on the desk—a shiny, fake antique thing loaded up with a messy pile of his mail and a large ashtray of change. I put the money down, one hundred and fifty bucks. He didn't want to touch it, like I said he was sweet, and so you could tell he didn't want to sully things by directly taking the money for what we were going to do.

He asked if I was gay or bi or straight. I told him I was straight, that I didn't have much experience, and what I wanted. "Take your clothes off," he said.

I did and he opened his robe and he had a gigantic cock. "Can you put a condom on?" I asked.

"No problem," he said.

He stroked himself to get hard. His body was heavier than his picture in the paper, but not by too much. When he was hard, he put a condom on, and he stayed sitting on the edge of his bed.

The thing was twice the size of mine and most women tell me I have a nice one. I don't know if they're lying or if this guy was unnatural. Once the condom was in place, I got on my knees and sucked it.

I could just about get the head in my mouth. It was thrilling for about the first minute and then it got dull. I felt a little ridiculous sucking this big rubbery thing.

We got on the bed. He took the condom off and spooned me. I asked him what his other clients were like. He said they were mostly married men. "Nice guys," he said. "A few regulars." We lay there silently. I felt small in his arms. It sort of reminded me of what I was trying to recreate, which made me feel a little sick, but I tried to get into it, to feel queer and all right with being held by a man. I wondered if this was how girls felt in my arms. I'm six-foot and bigger than all the girls I see.

"How old are you?" he asked.

"Thirty-two," I said.

"Just a baby," he said.

Then he lubed me up, put on a new condom, bent me over the edge of the bed, and somehow got the thing in there. "Please don't move," I said.

It hurt and then I got used to it, but it never felt good. I thought something might go wrong with my bowels, told him as much, and he pulled out. He washed up, put on his third condom of the night, and I sucked him some more, again kneeling on the floor. I masturbated my cock, which never got hard, but I came on a paper towel he had given me so as not to mess up his rug. He didn't come.

I stood up and he let me rinse off in the shower. His bathroom was small and a little cleaner than my own. He hugged me goodbye and gave me a kiss on the cheek.

"You're good looking," he said. "Next time you'll be more relaxed. We can enjoy each other more."

I got the hell out of there. I hated myself for about two hours, took a scalding bath back at my place, and then was able to sleep. The next day my ass was sore, but two days later it wasn't and I forgot about the whole thing.

Three years later I called him again.

It was around ten o'clock at night. I'd just had a date with a nice woman that had ended early and I was walking to the subway. Then I felt the insanity hit me. It's a combination of fierce loneliness and self-hate, and you need to do something to yourself right away to make it go away. It's like a mental cicada. I can go months, even years, without it happening, and then it's there.

So I found a *Village Voice*. I took it from one of the ubiqutous, battered red boxes, and it's a good thing they're all over the place so if you're hit by madness and have to find a prostitute right away to humiliate you it's not a lot of work. I went to the back pages and spotted his ad. I was pretty sure that it was his torso. There were a couple of other pictures of torsos, but I was sure that I remembered his specific ad.

It was a cold night and under a streetlight I was looking at the *Voice*, waiting for the sidewalk to be empty so nobody would know what I was doing (as if they would know or care, but shame makes you self-centered), and then I called his number on my cell-phone.

"I saw your ad," I said.

"Oh, yeah . . . When do you want to see me?"

"Now," I said.

He hesitated, then: "Okay. It's a cold night. I could use some warming up. Have I seen you before?"

"Yes," I said. "A few years ago."

"It's one-fifty. That all right?"

"Yeah, that's fine," I said.

"Well, it's freezing out. Let's make it one hundred."

I didn't know why he was lowering his price. Maybe he thought I wouldn't come. "Okay," I said.

"You remember my address?"

"Tell me again," I said.

I went to an ATM and got out two hundred dollars, then took a cab to his place. I remembered the staircase. I was trembling again. He opened the door a crack and then let me in. He was in the same robe and had a whiskey in his hand, but he had changed. His head was shaved and it didn't look good on him. His head was too large and the baldness made his skull look obscene. He had also put on about thirty pounds—now he definitely didn't resemble his ad. That may have been why he lowered the price.

"Do you remember me?" I asked.

He studied me. He seemed drunk. "I do," he said. "I remember your handsome face. But you never came back . . . Want a drink?"

"Just some water."

"Okay, take your clothes off, handsome, get comfortable."

I took off my clothes, except for my underwear, and sat on the edge of his bed. He brought me my water and sat next to me, sipped his whiskey.

"What do you do? What kind of work?" he asked. I hesitated a moment and he jumped in with: "You don't have to tell me. Or you can lie. It doesn't matter. Whatever you want."

He was hungry for conversation, lonely. He had lowered the price to insure I'd come over. I think he must have been drinking hard these last three years.

"I'm an actor," I said.

"You're in the arts," he said. "I love the arts. I wanted to be an artist."

I didn't say anything.

"I took a painting class in college," he continued, he was tipsy, slurring. "I loved it. I wanted to be a painter. I'd stay up all night painting. But this teacher, my first teacher, told me I was no good. He said I should be a hairdresser. I guess he could tell I was gay. It crushed me. I never recovered. But he was right. I was mediocre at best. You have to be great to be an artist. But I love creative things. Opera. Books. Movies. Paintings. I was in flowers. I might do it again. It's never too late. You never know."

"That wasn't fair of that teacher," I said.

"It wasn't meant to be," he said. He was full of clichés, but his story was heartbreaking.

Then he patted my knee. "Okay, good-looking."

He opened his robe. I got on my knees while he sat on the bed. I don't know why but this time I took the thing in my mouth without a condom. His big belly was just above me. I took my penis out of my boxer shorts and touched myself while he grew in my mouth. Again, I didn't get hard and I came almost immediately, maybe a minute after I had started. It was on the carpet. I stopped sucking him and we looked at the little drops on the floor.

"Don't worry about it," he said.

He went and got a paper towel and cleaned it up, which was nice of him, not asking me to do it. He put his robe back on and I started getting dressed. He watched me. He didn't ask but I put the money on his desk. I put one-hundred-and-fifty there. He'd count it after I left.

He hugged me goodbye. He smelled of the whiskey. "I like you," he said. "Don't be a stranger."

I raced down the stairs and went to a deli across the street. I bought a small bottle of green Listerine and then in the shadows of a doorway poured a bunch of it into my mouth and then spit. I repeated this several times, until I had used up the whole bottle. People walked past me as I spit out this green water but I didn't care. I had to make sure I killed all the germs. I did worry about him looking out the window and seeing me and feeling hurt, but I thought it was unlikely that he would spot me.

I got a cab and went home. That was two years ago. I have a feeling that guy is dead. Probably from drinking. But he was a nice guy. I wish that teacher hadn't crushed him.

Click

Jennifer Richter

There was no fire but everything beyond our back fence glowed. The sky was sirens: red, alive. Her father cut the grass that day then waited out the light and took his life. From my window in the dark I watched their crowded kitchen move. The girl ran screaming God into the yard past branches planted at her birth. The cardinal woke and sang What here? What here? Line up our families, before: we matched. The girl's arms thin as mine to pass a tiny broken eggshell through the fence. The red one singing birdie birdie birdie in his bandit mask thought only of himself. The gun hung on a nail behind her father's clothes. She wasn't meant to know. When the girl returned to Sunday school, the teacher startled, Oh! Hello! Let us start over, the teacher said. The girl refused to bow her head. The rest of us stared at the floor; we mumbled together Our father. The night he died I hid her in my house. I closed my closet door until it clicked. That night I was afraid of her.

Magic Word

They taught you only one. Only one works in the real world, one that sometimes gets you what you want. The others—long invented commands crowded with vowels—you kept to yourself. Your childhood nights wandered through woods; the downstairs clink and shush of company turned to the chirp and flutter of birds that led you through. You knew a shadowed door was hidden in the tallest oak; you knew the word to swing it open and go.

Years, and you're back. The forest is denser, darker than you remembered. Pain has branched through your body and rooted you. The wrens waiting in the clearing up ahead are your children. You want to be blinking back into their bright light but nothing you say works. All the shadows are you. You're collapsing like a kid, begging. You're back there. You're asking.

Recovery 2: Turn Away Your Eyes and It'll Fly

Pain stands you behind glass. A curiosity, a diagnosis, you inspire in everyone a circus of speculation. You are changed; they squint to see the measured you who speaks in meter, who doesn't grimace and grind her teeth like some beast.

Sometimes a flash of wings will crash into your glass then slump, shitting and shivering, staring, standing, now opening its mouth, its throat. The silence streaming out: a sound its loves aren't meant to hear. They'd hurt. You won't ever tell. This will happen to you again.

Relapse

Last year there were plenty of apples. And not wormy and chewed through. Now the tree is budding again, and your husband chooses today to prune the shooters. Then he hacks below the trunk's thick knots. Your daughter cries above the noise. Falling to the driveway are fists of gnarled bark. Wind lifts a few petals; today, another of your experts shrugged her shoulders. Everyone's sick of your story. At least all spring your kids will look at this instead of at you. Look at this. The truth is, you looked around all winter for something safe to damage.

Recovery 4

Each day you lay a few more things on the lawn. The way the neighbors pare down. The dozens of wobbling ladders in the grass: these are your doctor's long reports. The boxes labeled "Fragile": your nights awake. Your pills are the shoes, lined up in rows. A camper trailer on blocks: the public shape your grief has taken.

Your husband isn't sure he likes what's left. For years he was your shield: returning calls, muting the news, handing his heaviness to others. Your reactions have been flat as cut grass. Now you're striding through the empty rooms, swinging open doors. You're sweating. You don't want help. You're pressing past him, seeing at the last minute what you can't part with and rushing to it, out there.

Never remember how we got there
only how we left.

(Turner, page 123)

100 Visitors to the Biennial Immortalized

Ellen Harvey

This performance took place at the Park Avenue Armory as part of the 2008 Whitney Biennial, organized by Art Production Fund. The first one hundred people to sign up were offered free fifteen-minute pencil portraits in exchange for filling out questionnaires evaluating the success or failure of their portraits. At the end of the exhibition, all the portraits were scanned and the originals sent to the participants.

Photograph: Jan Baracz, 2008.

Number of Drawing: 73
Date:
Name (optional): AManda Drowder
Age (optional): 31

Why did you want a portrait?

I have never sat for a portrait before.

What do you think of your portrait in general? Do you think it looks like you?

I look very serious. which is funny because I laughed a lot
during the sitting.   Yes, I think it looks like me.

What do you think of the hair in your portrait?

I love my hair in the portrait. Very wavy

What do you think of the eyes / glasses in your portrait?

I think my glasses look very gothic. They are gold.

What do you think of the eyebrows in your portrait?

Maybe that is why I look so gothic.....my eyebrows are
hidden by my glasses. good to know!

What do you think of the nose in your portrait?

Reminds me of how I look like my sister.

What do you think of the mouth in your portrait?

Small + serious. Ha ha! I think I was nervous.

What do you think of the general shape of your face in the portrait?

I have great cheekbones.

What did you think of the experience of having your portrait drawn?

Nervey (Nerve-y) Tough business. But Ellen was so sweet
and it was great to hear about this project. I appreciate
how she is connecting w/ the public. Very generous.

Please make any additional comments:

I am curious how many people will frame these.
I am going to send this to my mom + dad, or grandpa.

Number of Drawing: 93
Date: 16 March 2008
Name (optional): Adrian Dannatt
Age (optional): —

Why did you want a portrait?

Because of the future

What do you think of your portrait in general? Do you think it looks like you?

Slightly through history

What do you think of the hair in your portrait?

Unutterable

What do you think of the eyes / glasses in your portrait?

beyond/host

What do you think of the eyebrows in your portrait?

arch

What do you think of the nose in your portrait?

to the point

What do you think of the mouth in your portrait?

Speakable

What do you think of the general shape of your face in the portrait?

necessary (broken)

What did you think of the experience of having your portrait drawn?

(test me) entirely right

Please make any additional comments:

trust enough

Number of Drawing: 52
Date: MARCH 12 2008
Name (optional): ELIZA PROCTOR
Age (optional): 45

— I APPRECIATE THE IRONY
OF RESIDING NEXT TO THE
FIRE EXTINGUISHER! YOU NEVER
CAN BE TOO SAFE ... FIRE
GUARD CERTIFIED FOR
475 KENT AVE
JANUARY 2008

Why did you want a portrait?

I WISHED TO SEE HOW you SEE (..ME..).

What do you think of your portrait in general? Do you think it looks like you? YES!

GREAT. ITS CAPTURED A MOMENT OF MY LIFE RIGHT
NOW —

What do you think of the hair in your portrait?

REALISTIC — DISHEVELED,

What do you think of the eyes / glasses in your portrait?

— VERY TRUE ... TIRED...(OF BEING HOMELESS).

What do you think of the eyebrows in your portrait?

REALISTIC ... BARELY NOTICABLE !

What do you think of the nose in your portrait?

UNFORTUNATELY REALISTIC ... PLEASE GIVE ME A ROMAN
NOSE ANY DAY,

What do you think of the mouth in your portrait?

SUPER . THX! MAKES ME FEEL THAT THIN LIPS
ARE "IN"

What do you think of the general shape of your face in the portrait?
NOT AS THIN/NARROW,
LOOKS MUCH MORE "NORMAL" THAN HOW I PICTURE
MYSELF.

What did you think of the experience of having your portrait drawn?
TOO SHORT BUT DEFINITLY
FUN — INFORMATIVE TO HEAR A BIT HOW LIFE
IS W/ A BABE — HOW EXHAUSTING BUT REWARDING
TO MANAGE YOUR WORK AT

Please make any additional comments: THE SAME TIME
SUPER HAPPY TO HAVE THIS
MOMENT OF LIGHTNESS
IN THE MIDST OF UNCERTAINTY — THANK YOU ELLEN !

Number of Drawing: 94
Date: 3/15/08
Name (optional): Victoria Manning
Age (optional): 28

Why did you want a portrait?

I think Ellen's work is great and secretly I've always wanted a portrait drawn of myself and never have. It's a fantastic project.

What do you think of your portrait in general? Do you think it looks like you?

Overall, I like the portrait. I find myself in the individual areas. My eyes look like my eyes; My lips look like my lips, etc. I'm not certain if it all comes together as me completely, though.

What do you think of the hair in your portrait?

The hair is very good - even captured the little wisps around my forehead.

What do you think of the eyes / glasses in your portrait?

I think the eyes were done very well, open and clear.

What do you think of the eyebrows in your portrait?

The eyebrows are very accurate - again the details of them kind of petering out at the ends.

What do you think of the nose in your portrait?

It is as narrow as mine. The nostril area may be a bit wide, or at least my perception of them is less wide.

What do you think of the mouth in your portrait?

My lips look good, a kind of tiny crooked section that I do have.

What do you think of the general shape of your face in the portrait?

This may be where all of the individualized accurate areas don't come together completely. I think my face might be less round. ▆ My cheekbones are usually more visible.

What did you think of the experience of having your portrait drawn?

It was ▆ different than I had expected. I didn't realize how much focus I was putting on how to stay still, when to talk, etc. I think it's really interesting that I have a mental portrait of Ellen's face permanently with me now.

Please make any additional comments:

Number of Drawing: 90
Date: 3/15/08
Name (optional): MARK MCGUIRE
Age (optional): 41

Why did you want a portrait?

IMMORTALITY COMES IN LITTLE BITS LIKE THIS.

What do you think of your portrait in general? Do you think it looks like you?

I ONLY HAVE ONE BROTHER, BUT IF I HAD ANOTHER
HE MIGHT LOOK LIKE THIS. AND IF HE WERE ANGRY.

What do you think of the hair in your portrait?

I THINK IT IS A MILDLY IRRITATING PROBLEM, JUST
LIKE IN REAL LIFE.

What do you think of the eyes / glasses in your portrait?

THEY ARE MY EYES! THE ONES I SEE WHEN I DARE TO LOOK.

What do you think of the eyebrows in your portrait?

I'D KNOW THOSE WISPY CRESCENTS ANYWHERE

What do you think of the nose in your portrait?

A NICE NOSE. A BOXER'S NOSE. A NOSE WITH CHARACTER.

What do you think of the mouth in your portrait?

IT'S ABOUT TO SNEER, BUT NOT AT THE ARTIST.

What do you think of the general shape of your face in the portrait?

THAT'S THE SHAPE MY FACE LIVES IN, MINUS (THANK YOU)
THE SAG.

What did you think of the experience of having your portrait drawn?

TWITCHY. BUT OKAY.

Please make any additional comments:

The Silver Christ of Santa Fe

Charles Bukowski

THEN I GOT A LETTER FROM MARX WHO HAD MOVED TO SANTA Fe. He said he'd pay trainfare and put me up if I came out for a while. He and his wife had a rent-free situation with this rich psychiatrist. The psychiatrist wanted them to move their printing press in there, but the press was too big to get into any of the doors, so the psychiatrist offered to have one of the walls smashed down to get the press in and then have the wall put back up. I think that's what worried Marx—having his beloved press locked in there like that. So Marx wanted me to come out and look at the psychiatrist and tell him if the psychiatrist was okay. I don't know quite how it got to be that way but I had been corresponding with this rich psychiatrist, who was also a very bad poet, for some time, but had never met him. I had also been corresponding with a poetess, a not very good poetess, Mona, and the next thing I knew the psychiatrist had divorced his wife and Mona had divorced her husband and then Mona had married the psychiatrist and now Mona was down there and Marx and his wife were down there and the psychiatrist's x-wife, Constance, was still on the grounds. And I was supposed to go down there and see if *everything* was all right. Marx thought I knew something. Well, I did. I could tell him that everything wasn't all right, you didn't have to be a sage to smell that one out but I guess Marx was so close to it, plus the rent-free situation, that he couldn't smell it. Jesus Christ. Well, I wasn't writing. I had written some dirty stories for the sex mags and had them accepted. I had a backlog of dirty stories accepted by the sex mags. So it was time for me to gather material for another dirty story and I felt sure there was a dirty story in Santa Fe. So I told Marx to wire the money . . .

The psychaitrist's name was Paul, if it matters.

I was sitting with Marx and his wife—Lorraine—and I was drinking a beer when Paul walked in with a highball. I don't know where he had come from. He had houses all over the hillside. There were four bathrooms with four bathtubs and four toilets to the door from the north. It simply appeared that Paul had walked out from the four-bathrooms with four bathtubs and four toilets with the cocktail in his hand. Marx introduced us. There was a silent hostility between Marx and Paul because Marx had allowed some Indians to bathe in one or more of the bathtubs. Paul didn't like Indians.

"Look, Paul," I asked, sucking at my beer, "tell me something?"

"What?"

"Am I crazy?"

"It'll cost you to find out."

"Forget it. I already know."

Then Mona seemed to walk out of the bathrooms. She was holding a boy in her arms from the other marriage, a boy of about three or four. They both had been crying. I was introduced to Mona and the boy. Then they walked away somewhere. Then Paul seemed to walk away with his cocktail glass.

"They hold poetry readings at Paul's place," said Marx. "Each Sunday. I saw the first one last Sunday. He makes them all line up single-file outside his door. Then he lets them in one by one and seats them and reads his own stuff first. He has all these bottles all over the place, everybody's tongue is hanging out for a drink but he won't pour one. Whatcha think of a son of a bitch like that?"

"Well, now," I said, "let's not get too hasty. Deep underneath all that crud, Paul might be a very fine man."

Marx stared at me and didn't answer. Lorraine just laughed. I walked out and got another beer, opened it.

"No, no, you see," I said, "it might be his money. All that money is causing some kind of block; his goodness is locked-in there, can't get out, you see? Now maybe if he got rid of some of his money he'd feel better, more human. Maybe everybody would feel better . . ."

"But what about the Indians?" Lorraine asked.

"We'll give them some too."

"No, I mean, I told Paul that I was going to let them keep coming up here and taking baths. And they can crap too."

"Of course they can."

"And I like to talk to the Indians. I like the Indians. But Paul says he doesn't want them around."

"How many Indians come around here everyday to bathe?"

"Oh, eight or nine. The squaws come too."

"Any young squaws?"

"No."

"Well, let's not worry too much about the Indians . . ."

The next night Constance, the x-wife came in. She had a cocktail glass in her hand and was a bit high. She was still living in one of Paul's houses. And Paul was still seeing her. In other words, Paul had two wives. Maybe more. She sat next to me and I felt her flank up against mine. She was around twenty-three and looked a hell of a lot better than Mona. She spoke with a mixed French-German accent.

"I just came from a party," she said, "everybody bored me to death. Leetle turds of people, phonies, I *just* couldn't stand it!"

Then Constance turned to me. "Henry Chinaski, you look *just* like what you write!"

"Honey, I don't write *that* badly!"

She laughed and I kissed her. "You're a very beautiful lady," I told her, "you are one of those class bitches that I'll go to my grave without ever possessing. There's such a gap, educational, social, cultural, all that crap—like age. It's sad."

"I could be your granddaughter," she said.

I kissed her again, my hands around her hips.

"I don't need any granddaughters," I said.

"I have something to drink at my place," she said.

"To hell with these people," I said, "let's go to your place."

"Very vell," she said.

I got up and followed her . . .

We sat in the kitchen drinking. Constance had on one of these, well, what could you call it? . . . one of these green peasant dresses . . . a necklace of white pearls that wound around and around and around, and her hips came in at the right place and her breasts came out at the right places and her eyes were green and she was blonde and she danced to music coming over the intercom—classical music—and I sat there drinking, and she danced, whirled, with a drink in her hand and I got up and grabbed her and said, "Jesus Christ Jesus Christ, I CAN'T STAND IT!" I kissed her and felt her all over. Our tongues met. Those green eyes stayed open and looked into mine. She broke off.

"VAIT! I'll be back!"

I sat down and had another drink.

Then I heard her voice. "I'm in here!"

I walked into the other room and there was Constance, naked, stretched on a leather couch, her eyes closed. All the lights were on, which only made it better. She was milk-white and *all* there, only the hairs of her pussy had a rather golden-red tint instead of the blonde like the hair on her head. I began to work on her breasts and the nipples became hard immediately. I put my hand between her legs and worked a finger in. I kissed her all about the throat and ears and as I slipped it in, I found her mouth. I knew I was going to make it at last. It was good and she was responding, she was wiggling like a snake. At last, I had my manhood back. I was going to score. All those misses . . . so many of them . . . at the age of fifty . . . it *could* make a man doubt. And, after all, what was a man if he couldn't? What did poems mean? The ability to screw a lovely woman was Man's greatest Art. Everything else was tinfoil. Immortality was the ability to screw until you died . . .

Then I looked up as I was stroking. There on the wall opposite to my sight hung a life-sized silver Christ nailed to a life-sized silver cross. His eyes appeared to be open and He was watching me.

I missed a stroke.

"Vas?" she asked.

It's just something *manufactured*, I thought, it's just a bunch of silver hanging on the wall. That's all it is, just a bunch of silver. And you're not religious.

His eyes seemed to grow larger, pulsate. Those nails, the thorns. The poor Guy, they'd murdered Him, now He was just a hunk of silver on the wall, watching, watching . . .

My pecker went down and I pulled out.

"Vas iss it? Vas iss it?"

I got back into my clothes.

"I'm leaving!"

I walked out the back door. It clicked locked behind me. Jesus Christ! It was raining! An unbelievable burst of water. It was one of those rains you knew wouldn't stop for hours. *Ice cold!* I ran to Marx's place which was next door and beat on the door. I beat and I beat and I beat. They didn't answer. I ran back to Constance's place and I beat and I beat and I beat.

"Constance, it's raining! Constance, my LOVE, it's raining, I'm DYING OUT HERE IN THE COLD RAIN AND MARX WON'T LET ME IN! MARX IS MAD AT ME!"

I heard her voice through the door.

"Go away, you . . . you rotten sune of a bitcher!"

I ran back to Marx's door. I beat and beat. No answer. There were cars parked all around. I tried the doors. Locked. There was a garage but it was just made out of slats; the rain poured through. Paul knew how to save money. Paul would never be poor. Paul would never be locked out in the rain.

"MARX, MERCY! I'VE GOT A LITTLE GIRL! SHE'LL CRY IF I DIE!"

Finally the editor of *Overthrow* opened the door. I walked in. I got a bottle of beer and sat on my couch-bed after taking off my clothes.

"You said, 'To hell with these people!' when you left," said Marx. "You can talk to me that way but you can't talk to Lorraine that way!"

Marx kept on with the same thing, over and over—you can't talk to my wife that way, you can't talk to my wife that way, you can't—I drank three more bottles of beer and he went on and on.

"For Christ's sake," I said, "I'll leave in the morning. You've got my train ticket. There aren't any trains running now."

Marx bitched a while longer and then he was asleep and I had a beer, a nightcap beer, and I thought, I wonder if Constance is asleep? . . . It rained.

Wild Berry Blue

Rivka Galchen

THIS IS A STORY ABOUT MY LOVE FOR ROY THOUGH FIRST I HAVE
to say a few words about my dad, who was there with me at the
McDonald's every Saturday letting his little girl—I was maybe
eight—swig his extra half and halfs, stack the shells into messy tow-
ers. My dad drank from his bottomless cup of coffee and read the
paper while I dipped my McDonaldland cookies in milk and pretended to read the paper. He wore gauzy plaid button-ups with
pearline snaps. He had girlish wrists, a broad forehead like a Roman,
and an absolutely terrifying sneeze.

"How's the coffee?" I'd ask.

"Not good, not bad. How's the milk?"

"Terrific," I'd say. Or maybe, "Exquisite."

My mom was at home cleaning the house; our job there at the
McDonald's was to be out of her way.

And that's how it always was on Saturdays. We were Jews, we had
our rituals. That's how I think about it. Despite the occasional guilt-
less cheeseburger, despite being secular Israelis living in the wilds of
Oklahoma, the ineluctable Jew part in us still snuck out, like an
inherited tic, indulging in habits of repetition. Our form of *daven-
ning*. Our little Shabbat.

Many of the people who worked at the McDonald's were former patients of my dad's: mostly drug addicts and alcoholics in rehab programs. McDonald's hired people no one else would hire; I think it was a policy. And my dad, in effect, was the McDonald's—Psychiatric Institute liaison. The McDonald's manager, a deeply Christian man, would regularly come over and say hello to us, and thank my dad for many things. Once he thanked him for, as a Jew, having kept safe the word of God during all the dark years.

"I'm not sure I've done *so* much," my dad had answered, not seriously.

"But it's been living there in you," the manager said earnestly. He was basically a nice man, admirably tolerant of the accompanying dramas of his work force, dramas I picked up on peripherally. Absenteeism, petty theft, a worker OD-ing in the bathroom. I had no idea what that meant, to OD, but it sounded spooky. "They slip out from under their own control," I heard the manager say one time, and the phrase stuck with me. I pictured one half of a person lifting up a velvet rope and fleeing the other half.

Sometimes, dipping my McDonaldland cookies—Fryguy, Grimace— I'd hold a cookie in the milk too long and it would saturate and crumble to the bottom of the carton. There, it was something mealy, vulgar. Horrible. I'd lose my appetite. Though the surface of the milk often remained pristine I could feel the cookie's presence down below, lurking, like some ancient bottom-dwelling fish with both eyes on one side of his head.

I'd tip the carton back slowly in order to see what I dreaded seeing, just to feel that queasiness, and also the prequeasiness of knowing the main queasiness was coming, the anticipatory ill.

Beautiful/Horrible—I had a running mental list. Cleaning lint from the screen of the dryer—beautiful. Bright glare on glass—horrible. Mealworms—also horrible. The stubbles of shaved hair in a woman's armpit—beautiful.

The Saturday I was to meet Roy, after dropping a cookie in the milk, I looked up at my dad. "Cookie," I squeaked, turning a sour face at the carton.

He pulled out his worn leather wallet, with its inexplicable rust stain ring on the front. He gave me a dollar. My mom never gave me money and my dad always gave me more than I needed. (He also called me the Queen of Sheba sometimes, like when I'd stand up on a dining room chair to see how things looked from there.) The torn corner of the bill he gave me was held on with yellowed Scotch tape. Someone had written over the treasury seal in blue pen, "I love Becky!!!"

I go up to the counter with the Becky dollar to buy my replacement milk, and what I see is a tattoo, most of which I can't see. A starched white long-sleeve shirt covers most of it. But a little blue-black lattice of it I can see—a fragment like ancient elaborate metalwork, that creeps down all the way, past the wrist, to the back of the hand, kinking up and over a very plump vein. The vein is so distended I imagine laying my cheek on it in order to feel the blood pulse and flow, to maybe even hear it. Beautiful. So beautiful. I don't know why but I'm certain this tattoo reaches all the way up to his shoulder. His skin is deeply tanned but the webbing between his fingers sooty pale.

This beautiful feeling. I haven't had it about a person before. Not in this way.

In a trembling moment I shift my gaze up to the engraved name tag. There's a yellow M emblem, then *Roy*.

I place my dollar down on the counter. I put it down like it's a password I'm unsure of, one told to me by an unreliable source. "Milk," I say, quietly.

Roy, whose face I finally look at, is staring off, up, over past my head, like a bored lifeguard. He hasn't heard or noticed me, little me, the only person on line. Roy is biting his lower lip and one of his teeth, one of the canines, is much whiter than the others. Along his cheekbones his skin looks dry and chalky. His eyes are blue, with beautiful bruisy eyelids.

I try again, a little bit louder. "Milk."

Still he doesn't hear me; I begin to feel as if maybe I am going to cry because of these accumulated moments of being nothing. That's what it feels like standing so close to this type of beauty—like being nothing.

Resolving to give up if I'm not noticed soon I make one last effort and, leaning over on my tiptoes, I push the dollar further along the counter, far enough that it tickles Roy's thigh, which is leaned up against the counter's edge.

He looks down at me, startled, then laughs abruptly. "Hi little sexy," he says. Then he laughs again, too loud, and the other cashier, who has one arm shrunken and paralyzed, turns and looks and then looks away again.

Suddenly these few seconds are everything that has ever happened to me.

My milk somehow purchased I go back to the table wondering if I am green, or emitting a high-pitched whistling sound, or dead.

I realize back at the table that it's not actually the first time I've seen Roy. With great concentration, I dip my Hamburglar cookie into the cool milk. I think that maybe I've seen Roy—that coarse blond hair— every Saturday, for all my Saturdays. I take a bite from my cookie. I have definitely seen him before. Just somehow, not in this way.

My dad appears to be safely immersed in whatever is on the other side of the crossword puzzle and bridge commentary page. I feel—a whole birch tree pressing against my inner walls, its leaves reaching to the top of my throat—the awful sense of wanting some other life. I have thought certain boys in my classes have pretty faces, but I have never before felt like laying my head down on the vein of a man's wrist. (I still think about that vein sometimes.) Almost frantically I wonder if Roy can see me there at my table, there with my dad, where I've been seemingly all my Saturdays.

Attempting to rein in my anxiety I try and think: What makes me feel this way? Possessed like this? Is it a smell in the air? It just smells like beefy grease, which is pleasant enough but nothing new. A little mustard. A small vapor of disinfectant. I wonder obscurely if Roy is Jewish, as if that might make normal this spiraling fated feeling I have. As if really what's struck me is just an unobvious family resemblance. But I know that we're the only Jews in town.

Esther married the gentile king, I think, in a desperate absurd flash.

Since a part of me wants to stay forever I finish my cookies quickly.

"Let's go," I say.

"Already?"

"Can't we just leave? Let's leave."

There's the Medieval Fair, I think to myself in consolation all Sunday. It's two weekends away, a Saturday. You're always happy at the Medieval Fair, I say to myself, as I fail to enjoy sorting my stamps, fail to stand expectantly, joyfully, on the dining room chair. Instead I fantasize about running the French fry fryer in the back of McDonald's. I imagine myself learning to construct Happy Meal boxes in a breath, to fold the papers around the hamburgers *just so*. I envision a stool set out for me to climb atop so that I can reach the apple fritter dispenser; Roy spots me, making sure I don't fall. And I get a tattoo of a bird, or a fish, or a ring of birds and fish, around my ankle.

But there is no happiness in these daydreams, just an overcrowded and feverish empty.

At school on Monday I sit dejectedly in the third row of Mrs. Brown's class, because that is where we are on the weekly seating chart rotation. I suffer through exercises in long division, through bits about Magellan. Since I'm not in the front I'm able to mark most of my time drawing a tremendous maze, one that stretches to the outer edges of the notebook paper. This while the teacher reads to us from something about a girl and her horse. Something. A horse. Who cares! Who cares about a horse! I think, filled, suddenly, with unexpected rage. That extra white tooth. The creeping chain of the tattoo. I try so hard to be dedicated to my maze, pressing my pencil sharply into the paper as if to hold down my focus better.

All superfluous, even my sprawling maze, superfluous. A flurry of pencil shavings from the sharpener—they come out as if in a breath—distracts me. A sudden phantom pain near my elbow consumes my attention.

I crumple up my maze dramatically; do a basketball throw to the wastebasket like the boys do. I miss of course but no one seems to notice, which is the nature of my life at school, where I am only noticed in bland embarrassing ways, like when a substitute teacher can't pronounce my last name. The joylessness of my basketball toss—it makes me look over at my once-crush Josh Deere and feel sad for him, for the smallness of his life.

One day, I think, it will be Saturday again.

But time seemed to move so slowly. I'd lost my appetite for certain details of life.

"Do you know about that guy at McDonald's with the one really white tooth?" I brave this question to my dad. This during a commercial break from *Kojak*.

"Roy's a recovering heroin addict," my dad says, turning to stare at me. He always said things to me other people wouldn't have said to kids. He'd already told me about the Oedipus complex and I had stared dully back at him. He would defend General Rommel to me, though I had no idea who General Rommel was. He'd make complex points about the straits of Bosporus. It was as if he couldn't distinguish ages.

So he said that to me, about Roy, which obviously he shouldn't have said. (Here, years later, I still think about the mystery of that plump vein, which seems a contradiction. Which occasionally makes me wonder if there were two Roys.)

"I don't know what the story with the tooth is," my dad adds. "Maybe it's false?" And then it's back to the mystery of *Kojak*.

I wander into the kitchen feeling unfulfilled and so start interrogating my mom about my Purim costume for the carnival that is still two Sundays, eons away. The Purim carnival is in Tulsa, over an hour's driving distance; I don't know the kids there, and my costume never measures up. "And the crown," I remind her hollowly. I'm not quite bold enough to bring up that she could buy me one of the beautiful ribbon crowns sold at the Medieval Fair, which we'll be at the day before. "I don't want," I mumble mostly to myself, "one of those paper crowns that everyone has."

Thursday night I am at the Skaggs Alpha Beta grocery with my mom. I am lingering amid all the sugar cereals I know will never come home with me. It's only every minute or so that I am thinking about Roy's hand, about how he called me sexy.

Then I see Roy. He has no cart, no basket. He's holding a gallon of milk and a supersized bag of Twizzlers and he is reaching for, I can't quite see—a big oversized box that looks to be Honeycomb. A beautiful assemblage. Beautiful.

I turn away from Roy but stand still. I feel my whole body, even my ears, blushing. The backs of my hands feel itchy the way they always do in spring. Seeking release I touch the cool metal shelving, run my fingers up and over the plastic slipcovers, over the price labels, hearing every nothing behind me. The price labels make a sandy sliding sound when I push them. He's a monster, Roy. Not looking at him, just feeling that power he has over me, a monster.

My mom in lace-up sandals cruises by the aisle with our shopping cart, unveiling to me my ridiculousness. Able now to turn around I see that Roy is gone. I run after my mom and when finally we're in the car again, backdoor closed on the groceries—I see celery stalks innocently sticking out of a brown paper bag when I turn around—I feel great relief.

I decide to wash my feet in the sink, this always makes me happy. On my dad's shaving mirror in the bathroom, old Scotch tape holding it in place, is a yellowed bit of paper, torn from a magazine. For years it's been there, inscrutable, and suddenly I feel certain that it carries a secret. About love maybe. About the possessed feeling I have because of Roy.

It says *And human speech is but a cracked kettle upon which we tap crude rhythms for bears to dance to, while we long to make music that—*

Next to the scrap is a sticker of mine, of a green apple.

I look again at the quote: the bears, the kettle.

Silly I decide. It's all very silly. I start to dry my feet with a towel.

For the impending McDonald's Saturday I resolve to walk right past my tattooed crush. I'll have nothing to do with him, with his hi little sexys. This denouncement is actually extraordinarily painful since Roy alone is now my whole world. Everything that came before—my coin collection in the Tupperware, the corrugated cardboard trim on school bulletin boards, the terror of the fire pole—now revealed supremely childish and vain. Without even deciding to, I have left all that and now must leave Roy too. I commit to enduring the burden of the universe alone. The universe with its mysterious General Rommels, its heady straits of Bosporus. I resolve to suffer.

Saturday comes again. My mom has already taken the burner covers off the stove and set them in the sink. I'm anxious, like branches shaking in wind, and I'm trying the think-about-the-Medieval-Fair trick. I picture the ducks at the duck pond, the way they waddle right up and snatch the bread slice right out of my hand. I focus on the fair—knowing that time will move forward in that way, eventually waddle forward to the next weekend.

Buckling myself into the front seat of our yellow Pinto, I put an imitation Lifesaver under my tongue, a blue one. When my dad walks in front of the car on the way to the driver's side, I notice that he has slouchy shoulders. Horrible. Not his shoulders, but my noticing them.

"I love you," I say to my dad. He laughs and says that's good. I sit there hating myself a little.

I concentrate on my candy, on letting it be there, letting it do its exquisitely slow melt under my tongue. Beautiful. I keep that same candy the whole car ride over, through stop signs, waiting for a kid on a Bigwheel to cross, past the Conoco, with patience during the long wait for the final left turn. In my pocket I have more candies. Most of a roll of wild berry. When I move my tongue just a tiny bit, the flavor, the sugary slur, assaults my sensations. I choke on a little bit of saliva.

When we enter I sense Roy at our left; I walk on the far side of my dad, hoping to hide in his shadow. In a hoarse whisper I tell my dad that I'll go save our table and that he should order me the milk and the cookies.

"Okay," he whispers back, winking, as if this is some spy game I am playing.

At the table I stare straight ahead at the molded plastic bench, summoning all my meager power to keep from looking feverishly around. I think I sense Roy's blond hair off in the distance to my left. I glimpse to the side, but see just a potted plant.

"How's the coffee?" I ask after my dad has settled in across from me.

He shrugs his ritual shrug but no words except the question of how is your milk. Is he mad at me? As I begin dipping my cookies with a kind of anguish I answer that the milk is delicious.

Why do we say these little things? I wonder. Why do I always want the McDonaldland butter cookies and never the chocolate chip? It seems creepy to me suddenly, all the habits and ways of the heart I have that I didn't choose for myself.

I throw back three half and halfs.

"Will you get me some more half and halfs?" my dad asks.

He asks nicely. And he is really reading the paper while I am not. Of course I'm going to go get creamers. I'm a kid, I remember. He's my dad. All this comes quickly into focus, lines sharp, like feeling the edges of a sticker on paper.

"I don't feel well," I try.

"Really?"

"I mean I feel fine," I say getting out of the chair.

Roy. Taking a wild berry candy from my pocket I resolve again to focus on a candy under my tongue instead of on him. I head first toward the back wall, darting betwixt and between the tables with their attached swiveling chairs. This is the shiniest cleanest place in town, that's what McDonald's was like back then. Even the corners and crevices are clean. Our house—even after my mom cleans it's all still in disarray. I'll unfold a blanket and find a stray sock inside. Behind the toilet there's blue lint. Maybe that's what makes a home, I think, its special type of mess.

And then I'm at the front counter. I don't look up.

I stand off to the side since I'm not really ordering anything, just asking for a favor, not paying for milk but asking for creamers. Waiting to be noticed, I stare down at the brushed steel counter with its flattering hazy reflection and then it appears, he appears. I see first his palm, reflected in the steel. Then I see his knuckles, the hairs on the back of his hand, the lattice tattoo, the starched shirt cuff that is the beginning of hiding all the rest of the tattoo that I can't see.

Beautiful.

A part of me decides I am taking him back into my heart. Even if no room will be left for anything else.

Roy notices me. He leans way down, eyes level with my sweaty curls stuck against my forehead, at the place where I know I have my birthmark—a dark brown mole there above my left eyebrow—and he says, his teeth showing, his strange glowing white canine showing—"Dya need something?" He taps my nose with his finger.

That candy—I had forgotten about it, and I move my tongue and the flavor—it all comes rushing out, overwhelming, and I drool a little bit as I blurt out, "I'm going to the Medieval Fair next weekend." I wipe my wet lips with the back of my hand and see the wild-berry blue saliva staining there.

"Cool," he says, straightening up, and he interlaces his fingers and pushes them outward and they crack deliciously, and I think about macadamias. I think I see him noticing the blue smeared on my right hand. He then says to me: "I love those puppets they sell there—those real plain wood ones."

I just stare at Roy's blue eyes. I love blue eyes. Still to this day I am always telling myself that I don't like them, that I find them lifeless and dull and that I prefer brown eyes, like mine, like my parents', but it's a lie. It's a whole other wilder type of love that I feel for these blue-eyed people of the world. So I look up at him, at those blue eyes, and I'm thinking about those plain wooden puppets—this is all half a second—then the doors open behind me and that invasive heat enters and the world sinks down, mud and mush and the paste left behind by cookies.

"Oh," I say. "Half and half."

He reaches into a tray of much melted ice and bobbing creamers and he hands three to me. My palm burns where he touched me and my vision is blurry; only the grooves on the half and half container keep me from vanishing.

"Are you going to the fair?" I brave. Heat in my face again, the feeling just before a terrible rash. I'm already leaving the counter so as not to see those awful blue eyes and I hear, "Ah I'm workin,'" and I don't even turn around.

I read the back of my dad's newspaper. They have found more fossils at the Spiro mounds. There's no explanation for how I feel.

How can I describe the days of the next week? I'd hope to see Roy when I ran out to check the mail. I'd go drink from the hose in our front yard thinking he might walk or drive by, even though I had no reason to believe he might ever come to our neighborhood. I got detention for not turning in my book report of *The Yellow Wallpaper*. I found myself rummaging around in my father briefcase, as if Roy's files—I imagined the yellow confidential envelope from Clue—might somehow be there. Maybe I don't need to explain this because who hasn't been overtaken by this monstrous shade of love? I remember walking home from school very slowly, anxiously, as if through foreign, unpredictable terrain. I wanted to buy Roy a puppet at the Medieval Fair. One of the wooden ones like he'd mentioned. Only in that thought could I rest. All the clutter of my mind was waiting to come closer to that moment of purchasing a puppet.

So I did manage to wake up in the mornings. I did try to go to sleep at night. Though my heart seemed to be racing to its own obscure rhythm, private, even from me.

Friday night before the fair, hopeless for sleep—my bedroom seemed alien and lurksome—I pulled my maze workbook from the shelf and went into the brightly lit bathroom. I turned on the overhead fan so that it would become noisy enough to overwhelm the sound in my mind of Roy cracking his knuckles, again and again. The whirring fan noise— it was like a quiet. I sat in the empty tub, set the maze book on the rounded ledge and purposely began on a difficult page. I worked cautiously, tracing ahead with my finger before setting pen to paper. This was pleasing, though out of the corner of my eye I saw the yellowed magazine fragment—*cracked kettle*—and through its message it was like a ghost in the room with me. I felt sure— almost too sure considering that I didn't understand it—it had nothing to do with me.

In the morning my mom found me there in the tub, like some passed out drunk, my maze book open on my small chest. I felt like crying, didn't even know why. I must have fallen asleep there. I reached up to my face, wondering if something had gone wrong with it.

"Do you have a fever?" my mom asked.

It must have seemed like there had to be an explanation. When she left, assured, somewhat, I tried out those words—*Human speech is like a cracked kettle*—like they were the coded answer to a riddle.

I was always that kind of kid who crawled into bed with her parents, who felt safe only with them. If my mom came into my classroom because I had forgotten my lunch at home, I wasn't ashamed like other kids were, but proud. For a few years of my life, up until then, my desires hadn't been chased away from me. I wanted to fall asleep on the sofa while my dad watched *The Twilight Zone* and so I did. I wanted couscous with butter and so I had some. Yes, sometimes shopping with my mom I coveted a pair of overalls or a frosted cookie, but the want would be faint and fade as soon as we'd walked away.

I had always loved the Medieval Fair. A woman would dress up in an elaborate mermaid costume and sit under the bridge that spanned the artificial pond. I thought she was beautiful. People tossed quarters down at her. She'd flap her tail, wave coyly. It wasn't until years later that I realized that she was considered trashy.

Further on there was a stacked hay maze that had already become too easy by late elementary school but I liked looking at it from a distance, from up on the small knoll. I think every turn you might take was fine. Whichever way you went you still made it out. I remember it being upsetting, being spat out so soon.

We had left the house uncleaned when we went to the fair that Saturday. I was thinking about the wooden puppet but I felt obligated to hope for a crown; that's what I was supposed to be pining for. I imagined that my mom would think to buy me a crown for my Queen Esther costume. But maybe, I hoped, she would forget all about the crown. It wasn't unlikely. What seemed like the world to me often revealed itself, through her eyes, to be nothing.

We saw the dress-up beggar with the prosthetic nose and warts. We crossed the bridge, saw the mermaid. A pale teenage boy in stonewashed jeans and a tanktop leaned against the bridge's railing, smoking, and looking down at her. Two corseted women farther along sang bawdy ballads in the shade of a willow and while we listened a slouchy man went by with a gigantic foam mallet. The whole world, it seemed, was laughing or fighting or crying or unfolding chairs or blending smoothies and this would go on until time immemorial. Vendors sold wooden flutes, Jacob's ladders. The smell of funnel cakes and sour mystery saturated the air. In an open field two ponies and three sheep were there for the petting and the overseer held a baby pig in his hands. We ate fresh ears of boiled corn, smothered with butter and cracked pepper. My mom didn't mention the price. That really did make it feel like a day in some other me's life.

But I felt so unsettled. Roy's tooth in my mind as I bit into the corn, Roy's fingers on my palm as I thrummed my hand along a low wooden fence. I had so little of Roy and yet he had all of me and the feeling ran deep, deep to the most ancient parts of me. So deep that in some way I felt that my love for Roy shamed my people, whoever my people were, whoever I was queen of, people I had never met, nervous people and sad people and dead people, all clambering for air and space inside of me. I didn't even know what I wanted from Roy. I still don't. All my life love has felt like a croquet mallet to the head. Something absurd, ready for violence. Love.

I remember once years later, in a love fit, stealing cherry Luden's cough drops from a convenience store. I had the money to pay for them but I stole them instead. I wanted a cheap childish cherry flavor on my tongue when I saw my love, who of course isn't my love anymore. That painful pathetic euphoria. Low quality cough drops. That's how I felt looking around anxiously for the wooden puppet stand, how I felt looking twice at every blonde man who passed wondering if he might somehow be Roy, there for me, even though he'd said he wouldn't be there. Thinking about that puppet for Roy eclipsed all other thoughts put a slithery veil over the whole day. How much would the puppet cost? I didn't have my own pocket money, an allowance or savings or anything like that. I wasn't in the habit of asking for things. I never asked for toys. I never asked for sugar cereals. I felt to do so was wrong. I had almost cried that one day just whispering to myself about the crown. But all I wanted was that puppet because that puppet was going to solve everything.

At the puppet stand I lingered. I was hoping that one of my parents would take notice of the puppets, pick one up. My dad, standing a few paces away, stood out from the crowd in his button-up shirt. He looked weak, sunbeaten. My mom was at my side, her arms crossed across an emergency orange tanktop. It struck me, maybe for the first time, that they came to this fair just for me.

"I've never wanted anything this much in my whole life," I confessed in a rush, my hand on the unfinished wood of one of the puppets. "I want this more than a crown."

My mom laughed at me, or at the puppet. "But it's so ugly," she said in Hebrew.

"That's not true," I whispered furiously, feeling as if everything had fallen silent, as if the ground beneath me was shifting. The vendor must surely have understood my mom, by her tone alone. I looked over at him: a fat bearded man talking to a long-haired barefoot princess. He held an end of her dusty hair distractedly; his other hand he had inside the collar of his shirt. He was sweating.

"*Drek*," my mom shrugged. Junk.

"Grouch," I broke out, like a tree root heaving through soil. "You don't like anything," I almost screamed, there in the bright sun. "You never like anything at all." My mother turned her back to me. I sensed the ugly vendor turn our way.

"I'll get it for you," my dad said, suddenly right with us. There followed an awkward argument between my parents, which seemed only to heighten my dad's pleasure in taking out his rust-stained wallet, in standing his ground, in being, irrevocably, on my side.

His alliance struck me as misguided, pathetic, even childish. I felt like a villain. We bought the puppet.

That dumb puppet—I carried it around in its wrinkly green plastic bag. For some reason I found myself haunted by the word leprosy. When we watched the minstrel show in the little outdoor amphitheater I tried to forget the green bag under the bench. We only made it a few steps before my mom noticed it was gone. She went back and fetched it.

At home I noticed that the wood of one of the hands of the puppet was cracked. That wasn't the only reason I couldn't give the puppet to Roy. Looking at that mute piece of wood I saw something. A part of me that I'd never chosen, that I would never control. I went to the bathroom, turned on the loud fan, and cried, feeling angry, useless, silly. An image of Roy came to my mind, particularly of that tooth. I felt my love falling off, dissolving.

He was my first love, my first love in the way that first loves are usually second or third or fourth loves. I still think about a stranger in a green jacket across from me in the waiting room at the DMV. About a blue-eyed man with a singed earlobe who I saw at a Baskin Robbins with his daughter. My first that kind of love. I never got over him. I never get over anyone.

The Girl in the Fake Leopard-Skin Coat

Said Shirazi

I.

I FIRST MET HER OUT IN SAN FRANCISCO—YOU KNOW, PALM trees, rolling hills to murder clutch and brakes, and row upon row of pastel Victorians like the one I had moved into with no plan soon after graduation. It was the right town for that at least. You could walk past all your friends' places in twenty minutes and half would be home, and if they'd had their burrito early would still come along for yours.

Back then the city was under gay martial law. Everyone knew some men had no interest in women but no one was permitted to believe there were guys who did not secretly like men. Homosexuality was celebrated from the rooftops but the existence of heterosexuality was considered an uncertain possibility at best. Among the people I knew saying you were definitely straight would have immediately established you as a liar and the secret accomplice of historical oppression: it would have meant you were the one who gave the Indians smallpox blankets and whipped raw the backs of the slaves. Such unforgivable arrogance would have made you a target at parties, someone to be prodded and provoked, so you had to be a sport about it sometimes.

Today it's mostly stoners with PlayStations but back then it was not yet an industry town, its main product not source code but an individual aura of righteousness. To be queer was most righteous, to be black or Latino next-to-most righteous, and bringing up the rear were white vegetarians, the unemployed, Asians, junkies, and only last, mysteriously least here, Jews.

But even for straights it was a golden age. At my peak I had three girlfriends. One knew about one of the others, one knew everything and one knew nothing. I wasn't even jealous when the first got a girlfriend of her own because there was no dick involved, possibly a failure of imagination on my part.

For weeks my friend Minsky had been telling me about this new girl who was really into him, but he was afraid of catching something from her. He was one of those guys who would never say he was into a girl, he would always say the girl was into him. I don't know whether one could have explained unrequited love to the infant Minsky even with puppets and a song, whether catching him at a formative age you could have given him the slightest inkling of why it had been supposed for so long to be noble. He was not here to sigh and suffer, he was here to reap the nubile bounty of the earth, like Bounty, a quicker picker-upper. I had seen him get numbers at a salad bar.

He took me along to meet her one night, for advice or to show her off, I don't know which. She was hanging out with a bunch of friends watching *The Texas Chainsaw Massacre* at her boyfriend's place. As we walked in she was bragging about having had every known STD at least once, with the obvious exception. During the movie she turned to me and asked what I thought of it and I told her it was a piece of crap. She said it was more fun to rent a bad movie and make fun of it than to get a good one.

I don't think I saw her again until the night she and her roommates threw a big party. It was early in the disco revival and everybody bobbed and stomped until the cops came twice, after which the hardcore revellers headed over to the Casa Loma bar, where she and

I had a second conversation almost as brief as our first. I had recently shaved my head and she was telling me I looked like Mayakovsky, the great Soviet poet, which was ridiculous. A few minutes later I heard her telling another guy the same thing. At least he had the build, but Mayakovsky hadn't cropped his hair to finesse a spreading scalp.

II.

In New York no one I know has sex, single or married. Instead they write articles full of recycled sex tips for glossy magazines. Everyone's faking it, trying to be the animals Freud said we were. I have friends who haven't had sex for five years, and that was once. I myself have gone two years and then a third right after that, and not for lack of trying.

I hustled up a fair number of dates for a guy with no money but I just couldn't make anything stick. I was always the wrong man for the job, too much bold and not enough persistent, and like anyone, I was selfish. I thought that I too deserved the best without even having decided for myself what was good.

I was talking to Strauss on the phone one day and he mentioned he had run into her with some guy at a little jazz club in the meat-packing district. After we hung up I got her new number from information and left a neighborly message with my number on her machine. Nothing happened. First me, then Strauss, and now her, sooner or later everyone gave up on California, for the same reasons they came. They started to feel guilty about the weather or the lack of it, and guilty about the lack of guilt.

Then one day she called. She said she had been out of town and had written my number down wrong and so on, and we agreed to meet the next day at the Astor Place Barnes & Noble, my least favorite spot in the world but just halfway between us and thus irresistibly convenient. I hate that there is no way to exit that place without walking through the middle of the café section, running a blind gauntlet of poseurs. I was always terrified of running into someone though I could never figure out who it might be.

When she arrived I saw she had brought her friend Adam along, the other Mayakovsky from the bar that night. It didn't bother me; I like clear signals. It would have been clear enough that we were going to keep some distance between us from the fact that we were having coffee during the afternoon instead of drinks at night.

She was wearing a fake leopard-skin coat and red plastic glasses, a hipster parody of tackiness. I told her that I was temping and my dad helped with my rent and she said that was her situation too. Afterward she had an errand to run and Adam and I both tagged along. We followed her to the Kinko's across the street to fax a copy of her driver's license to a real estate agent for an apartment she was applying for, but the number was busy. I offered to send it for her that evening since I had a fax machine at home.

Even in a slack, affectless license photo, her face was striking. It reminded me of Catherine Deneuve looking over her shoulder on the poster for *Belle du Jour,* her features frozen with dullness or caution but still alive, an undamaged human vessel seeking possession. The hologram of the California state seal hung in the laminate over her face like a glittering cloud of Disney dream dust.

I noticed we had been born on the same day but chose not to say anything about it. I wasn't sure how close I wanted to be either.

The next time we had coffee, Adam wasn't there; I was the only Mayakovsky. We met at the Café Orlin and talked for more than an hour about jazz and the prison system and the people from her high school who had gone to my college. She mentioned her roommate was meeting her there but said I didn't have to leave, in fact she was going with him to the studio to hear his jazz show and I was welcome to come along. I got nothing but dirty looks from the guy from the minute he walked in, which was fine since I hadn't wanted to go.

We started meeting during the day to write, first at cafés and then at our apartments. I knew we wouldn't get anything done; in my mind I counted it as a day off. Comparing our favorite writers, she found it odd that mine were all so personal when I myself seemed cold and distant.

As for herself, she liked French writers like Bataille and Genet. Her shelves were full of the unread theory she had shoplifted over the years. I told her I'd been through all that long ago and it was a bunch of worthless garbage. Theory, which tells us we have no access to reality . . . Theory, which tells us an alien language creates us . . . Theory, which says we are not responsible for our actions . . .

She was as sleek as an eel and sashimi cool, and always ready to laugh in your face a little. The first time I came over to her place, she had answered the door in sweats and no make-up, apologizing for her appearance. When I told her I preferred her this way she laughed at me. *You would*, she said disparagingly.

Soon she had opened up her shoebox of photos and was introducing me to the family. They didn't have money but according to her they had "cultural capital," a polite way for the educated to say they would rather be rich. I also got to meet her last few ex-boyfriends, all scrawny scowlers with bad bedhead, a definite type and one I fit so well that it occurred to me like Joseph in the house of Potiphar to leave my coat and flee.

Up close there was the slightest suggestion of poultry in her complexion and hints of a clamminess under her lightly powdered face. She was the kind of white girl I felt sorry for, the kind who felt they needed an alibi and so went out of their way to date minorities or lesbians to be interesting.

I kept insisting I could only get work done at home. The next time we met, she came over to my apartment and lay on my bed reading while I sat in a chair with a notepad. She looked over my few fledgling Coltrane albums and sneered, *What is this, Jazz 101?* After a respectable interval of feigned concentration, I climbed onto the bed next to her and she quickly suggested we go out to a café.

We went to Café dell'Artista and sat all the way in the back in a tiny room with double doors. She kept getting up to close the doors for privacy and the waiter kept coming back and opening them again. It didn't help that we hadn't ordered anything.

There's something I have to tell you, she said. But apparently she wasn't quite ready to tell me. Instead she dipped her finger in the sugar bowl and with a meaningful look in my direction sucked on it. *Now you do it*, she said. I took her finger, dipped it and sucked on it, though I knew she had meant for me to use my own; her eyes lit up with delight at the liberty. *I want to tell you*, she went on, *but I'm afraid you'll get mad. I want you to guess.*

I gently kissed her hand, warm in mine. *I'm not going to guess*, I said. *If there is anything you want me to know, you can just tell me what it is. You don't have to worry.* This went back and forth some time with neither of us yielding. Finally I decided to put a stop to the game by revealing that I already knew her secret, for I thought I did.

What is it, she demanded.

I wasn't sure how to put it. *That you used to… that you used to work as a prostitute*, I said.

What, she exploded. *No, that's not it.* She was perhaps most beautiful when she was surprised. Sometimes when she was surprised or tired, she stopped playing and pretending and I just really liked her. Her natural self would show through, an exciting and down-to-earth person, winningly sly and sharp. *I mean, I did*, she said, *but that's not what I'm talking about. Who told you that anyway?* Reluctantly I gave you up, Minsky. She considered for a moment, her eyes narrowed spitefully as if plotting revenge. *I know who told him*, she said at last. *No, that's not it at all. That's not a terrible secret*, she said. *In fact, it probably turns you on, doesn't it?*

The best I could do for her was to say I didn't know. *No*, she said, *no, no, no. No, my secret is that I have a boyfriend. That guy I introduced as my roommate is actually my boyfriend.*

Uh, yeah, I kinda figured, I said with a little snort. *But that's not a terrible secret either.* We still hadn't ordered anything; the waiter kept checking in. *And anyway, it's none of my business if you have a boyfriend.* She seemed a little embarrassed, her mouth puckering like an actress who can't bring up her next line. *I mean, is it?* I asked. *I can't imagine it would be.* She gave me a pleading look, waiting for help. *Unless . . . you like me?* I said.

I even think she blushed.

She went home after that but a few days later she called and invited me to the Fez with a bunch of her friends. Adam was there, he had just seen a documentary about Cocteau during the occupation, and discussing it they agreed they both would have probably collaborated. She turned and asked what I would have done.

I think America today is an occupied country, I said. *It's occupied by the forces of capitalism, and my refusal to get a job is a refusal to collaborate.* She looked at me with a mix of horror and admiration. After all the trouble she had gone through to drag Adam along, now she wanted to get rid of him.

Once she had, she took my hand and placed it behind her for me to feel the silk of her slip, which I rubbed a moment politely before withdrawing. She took my hand and placed it there again, waiting for me to understand. Then she raised her skirt a little to show a red garter. *Don't you get it*, she finally said, impatient with my obtuseness, *I'm not wearing any underwear.* Of two minds, she had gotten dressed up for me down there, dressed and undressed at the same time.

We left the bar and made out in one of the poster alcoves outside Tower Records, with the pantheon of rock radio looking on in back-lit approval. She took my index finger and slipped it up inside her like a dipstick. *Feel how wet I am*, she said, herself surprised. I couldn't persuade her to come home with me because her boyfriend was waiting up. Finally I got her to agree to a coin toss, which I lost.

The next time we met she sat in my chair and I lay back on the bed and before I had even started trying to think of some way to get a vibe going she leaned forward and said, *I really want to suck your dick but I can't because I have a Herpes sore.*

Instead she came a little closer and we lay on the bed together reading. After a few minutes, she suggested we read aloud to each other. I picked up Wallace Stevens from my bedside table while she went into the other room to get down the Marquis de Sade.

Just before she began, she turned over and lay across me so her breasts were pressing down on my groin. As she read, I started to lift my hips and thrust against her, basically dry-humping her chest. I wasn't even listening to the lubricious gymnastics the text described in such arcane detail; in fact, it would have been more exciting if she were reading government specifications or the *Herald-Tribune*, something from a world in which sex did not exist.

Right before I came, I lifted her skirt and looked underneath. Her pussy was like some rampant infection past all hope of treatment, an urban sprawl uncoiling in all directions. It seemed I glimpsed hair the color of dark honey running all the way up her belly and down her thighs like vines on an ancient ruined temple, bush as wild as the lawn in front of a dead or lunatic neighbor's house.

She was mad at my forwardness and surprised I could come from just a few minutes of friction, but she was also inexplicably hooked. *I've decided I want to do it*, she said as she was leaving, sounding a little like someone confirming an order for new curtains. *I've decided I want to have the affair.*

III.

Her sex was professional, like magazine fiction. From habit or preference she screwed without kissing. She always tried to put me off a while, maybe feeling guilty about her boyfriend, maybe trying to keep herself in check or just trying to make it last. Her sex voice was like another personality, high, cooing, and babyish. She would squirm and squeal not just during sex but sometimes switching over in the middle of an ordinary conversation. I knew before she told me that she would love being called Princess, it thrilled her and made her purr, as did Precious and Kitten.

As fake as she was sometimes, she taught me a thing or two about the real world. I hadn't realized that all of the escort services in the phone book were prostitution. I assumed that some above-the-board companies existed to provide cover for the others. Of course there is no such thing as a legitimate escort, no businessman from out of town ever needs to hire a beautiful stranger as his dinner companion in order to keep up appearances at an event. It is appearances that require he dine alone.

I also hadn't known that most prostitutes charge by time, not act. A respectable woman will make a man pay for every increment of her favors, every stage of her unwilling descent into the humiliation of sensuality, but to a pro it's just how long you keep her from being on her way.

She didn't have a pimp, just an agency like me, but with shorter assignments and better pay. I'll never know if she considered it a lie that first day when she told me she was temping too. She charged the going rate for a classy operation, three hundred an hour or a thousand for the whole night. Half was supposed to go to the agency but she was clever enough to cut them out. If she trusted a regular client she would give him her home number, but she would also have him still call the agency sometimes and ask for her when she wasn't available so they wouldn't suspect anything.

A lot of the guys just wanted someone to talk to or do drugs with or they got so fucked up on drugs beforehand that they forgot about the sex. Sometimes they even sent her out to buy the drugs, which was more dangerous.

She was surprised I had never gone to a prostitute because I seemed like the type to her. *Do you experience contempt after ejaculation?* she asked once afterward. Usually I felt gratitude but somehow not with her. I seemed cold to her and she seemed cold to me. Maybe a cold core was what allowed her to have numb sex and then collect for it, or maybe she was shivering inside and had to rub up to try to stay warm.

In her own mind she was a rebel, as if sex were power, as if sex were anything but tension and release, a close-range archery of the flesh. She wanted her sex to be a political statement, a revolutionary discipline like self-criticism or reeducation, as if you could flop your way to freedom on the thin raft of a dirty bedsheet, as if just having a crack in it somehow put her ass up there with the Liberty Bell.

Sex was the whole of her personality, the itch and fire of it, but I didn't get the sense she fucked a lot of people. Strangers, yes, and yes, for money, but off the clock she really wasn't loose. She was intense, a little fierce even, a woman who took a lover and dreamed of serving him as loyally as Jeannie did her astronaut master. *None of my boyfriends ever use a condom*, she said proudly; that was how she knew it was love.

I saw her as a kind of sorcerer's apprentice; she had tried to win power through sex but the spell turned and threatened to consume her. Years ago in the shower, an old girlfriend of mine had lain down with her legs spread so the water streaming off my limp dick would land on her clit and tickle it. For ten minutes she lay there twisting in the tub, wrestling her private angel of pleasure beneath this improvised fountain while I stood wondering. Her pussy was like a leech that would draw vital strength away until she blacked out, a barbaric bleeding that could kill as easily as cure. It was like a handle by which anyone might reach over and lift her. Sex can rush in and take over and turn you so entirely inward that you don't even know there's someone else in the room. I saw her in the thrall of it, so lost in herself that she no longer had any concept of persons. I watched her moving crazed in a glorious isolation.

IV.

Every man is a king with his dick up someone's ass, a young Arthur resheathing his Excalibur with each stroke. Hers was as full and taut in its skin as the padding of a boxing glove. When I pressed myself against it, it would start to quiver and tremble, a Mexican jumping bean, a Magic Fingers motel mattress. Sometimes having sex with her I felt like the statue of a hero in a public park. I felt exemplary, defiant, as if sex had been forbidden and I were openly breaking an unjust law, a patriot throwing crates of tea into the harbor. Standing behind her as she bent over the sink, I felt a kind of coursing civic glory, through Greek love attaining a Roman virtue.

Whenever we were close I pushed myself toward her like one magnet trying to flip another.In time our sexual bargaining fell into a routine. I would press against her from behind and whisper that I wanted to fuck her in the ass, she would protest and offer to suck my dick instead, and after some hesitation I would accept.

The greatest irony of our sexual etiquette is the consolation blowjob. To a woman it is less intimate and so feels less like cheating; for a guy it's double-pay for calling in sick. And I bet her boyfriend would have rather heard she screwed a guy than blew him, because opening your lips seems more of an act of submission than opening your legs, as if there were still a chance that while getting screwed she might have been giving his rival a steely and dubious look up top, not quite buying the performance.

Sexual sensation is intense because it is unfocused; ecstasy is always unclear. Being in a woman's mouth is like sinking into a warm bath, pleasure everywhere and nowhere at once, even though for all you know she might just be pumping you with a spit-slick hand, a whore's trick but one every wife should know. Even in the near-total passivity of having your dick sucked, there is a residual amount of anxiety because you're supposed to get stiff and applaudingly come and sometimes you just can't, which can be frustrating, though most of the time the woman blames herself, either her skill or more hurtfully her general excitingness.

One night she called to try to get me to go to a party; her boyfriend was going to be there but she wanted to sneak into the bathroom and suck me off. Another time she and I were writing together and she grabbed the page out of my hand and started reading. She began raving unconvincingly before she could have even finished the page, saying she wanted to suck my dick every day for however long it took me to get famous.

Blowjob was like the Name of Our Lord to her. To express appreciation she offered a lifetime supply. It was as if she had discovered a private currency she could print in the basement in great counterfeit wads.

She was even broker than I was. Her boyfriend had been paying her share of the rent and groceries for months. Meanwhile she complained of his dullness to me as if she were inherently interesting and the fact that she could go out with someone as dull as him was only one more fascinating thing about her. She had borrowed money from all her friends. She owed the other Mayakovsky thousands of rubles I knew he'd never see again.

She still worked occasionally. She tried to get me to come along one time when an old client wanted a video of her with another girl and she needed someone to hold the camera. Once she called me feeling depressed after a trick and we met at the Greenwich Café. I didn't think anything would happen afterward because it didn't seem like sex would cheer you up under the circumstances, but we went back to my place and afterward she seemed much happier. I put on a condom and pushed myself inside and came so fast she thought I hadn't even gotten hard. *Vidi, veni, vici:* I saw, I came, I conked out.

I think it was for the same client that she went out to someone's country house and had herself videotaped blowing a horse. She petted him awhile and then crouched down and opened her throat greedily to gorge herself, as if sensing his bestial form were only some pagan god's latest ruse. At one point a little girl wandered into the stables and amazingly no one thought to stop what they were doing and get her out until it was over. Afterward they panicked that the child might let something slip and so they erased the tape to get rid of the evidence. She was furious about losing the money. She was only telling me this for sympathy, her day's work having been ruined, but hearing it I felt as if the real self I thought I had glimpsed was entirely imaginary and her fakeness all there really was.

If the poor horse was a little confused during all this, I knew how he felt. After blowing me she would run to the bathroom and spit my seed out into the sink. Then she would preen and prance around the room like a touchdown receiver in the end zone. She often complained about the taste, asking what I'd been eating. *Did you eat hot dogs from a street vendor?* she would ask , making a face at the thought of something so disgusting. Usually she began praising her skills as soon as I was out of her mouth. *Don't I give the best blowjobs ever?* she would ask eagerly. *Not really*, I felt compelled to say, but quietly so as not to seem too ungracious.

Head is so much better when it comes from the heart. I'd had good sex and bad sex, cold sex and hot, but I'd never really had such bad hot sex before. I used to go around saying that there was no such thing as good sex, never really sure what I meant, maybe just that getting off pretty much always feels good and that's good enough for me, or maybe that I don't trust the kind of people who are always talking about good sex. In my experience, they turn out to be the worst.

V.

A lazy affair like this one is mostly a running argument over who has to come over to the other's apartment. When the argument's over, it means the affair is over. It wasn't long before we reached a point where neither of us was willing to budge. We'd talk on the phone and she would agree to come over and then after waiting an hour or two writhing on the futon I would call and she still wouldn't have left yet.

Having the same birthday cancelled the mental calculation I usually performed when talking to girls of trying to adjust for their age. We were both twenty-seven years, six months, and nine days old, so if she did something that I felt was immature then she was just immature.

A relationship is the only contest I know in which the one who quits first wins. But maybe I was playing the wrong game and by some other reckoning actually lost. Maybe I shouldn't have had anything to do with her in the first place or maybe I should have tried to make her change her ways. Maybe I could have understood her better than I did or even been able to finally learn something about myself. Maybe the will is really the ultimate weakness and winning is always a kind of losing.

It's rare that I can stand to be around someone in love with me. Every searching look feels like a year peeled off my life.

Let's try an experiment, I said, after a particularly annoying conversation. *You don't call me, and we'll see how long it takes for me to call you.* The idea of course was never, not that I thought I would make it. But days lined up into weeks and weeks marched by as months and to my surprise I found that I had done it, I had moved on, I had given her up for good.

Who strokes her white cheek now I do not know.

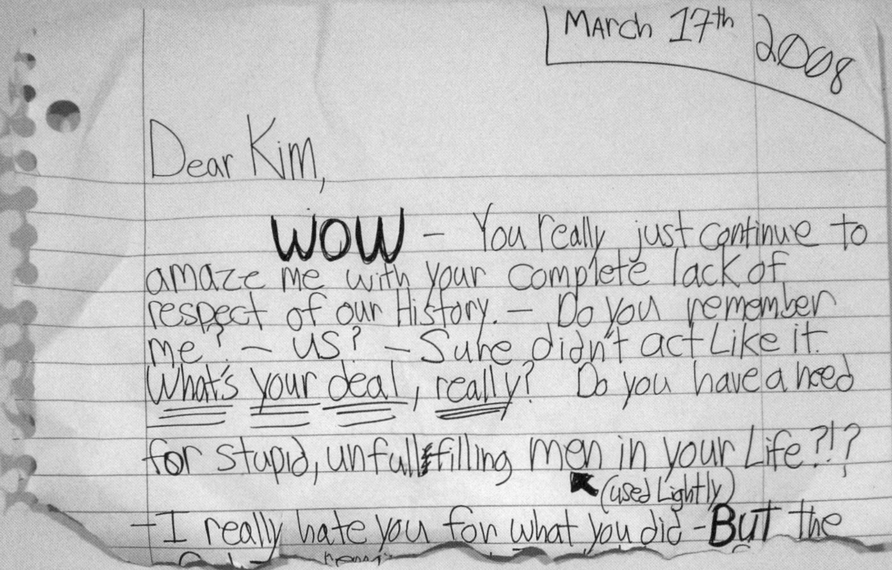

Drawings

Michael Scoggins

My List of Regrets   Michael S.

1) I Regret keeping my thoughts to myself.

2) I Regret getting drunk to escape our problems.

3) I Regret raising my voice.

4) I Regret being hard-headed.

5) I Regret putting my career first.

6) I Regret not talking about my feelings.

7) I Regret that I didn't always give you priority.

8) I Regret letting you take advantage of my kindness and trust.

9) I Regret you acting like a bitch.

10) I Regret letting you walk away.

11) I Regret how you ignored all our history.

12) I Regret feeling like I threw away two years of my life.

My Days in Exile [Day 77]

So, the evening started very well, I'm feeling better, trying to move on with my life. The Last few months have been pure **HELL!** a lot of crazy shit has transpired and I'm feeling spent...... Joel and I met at his place, we are shooting the video tonight and we were going to the bar to meet our friends..... We have some drinks and document and interview everyone for the piece.

It started off very well, Lots of people show up and we start to get buzzed............. **TheN**

<u>You fucking show UP</u> — what the hell?!? I try to ~~~~ it. I tell myself "You are working, let it go and do your job, don't let her ignore ruin this."

Then you start to hit on MY friend !!!! Bitch touching, flirting, Laughing that "cackle" you call a laugh (my friends use to ask me how I deal with your howling) I'm sitting across the table you Bitch !! This is my friend that I've know Longer than YOU. What is wrong with you, show some respect for fucksake. My brain is running, booze induced thoughts of pain and hate rage in me. I want to smack you, throw a glass at you — That's not me — <u>what have you done?</u>

Michael S.

The I.T. is My Bar, my hangout and you know this !

The Journal of Michael S
(zip pee de do)

And it's still Raining.

What a God damn Day. Man I'm so fed up with thing. You know, One of those days that you should have never gotten up. Everything is a fucking test and I've failed every mother fucking one. I really am full of Hate and I've given in and stopped trying to look at the brighter side. I've been sick for months now. A perpetual Illness. God's got a wicked sense of humor. Stress makes my head and chest ache. Just don't know any more.... fun times seemed to pass a long time ago. I mean, when did it all become a job? It use to be so different Have I changed? sure, but so has everyone else. Don't want to go outside, Lonely and bothered at the exact same time.... WHAT The HeLL? The crazy must be setting in... don't think I want to ride this ride any more.

I don't think she realizes that she really hurts me sometimes. I just want her to listen, I mean really listen.

...use to be a team, Right?

January 15th 2008

Michael S.

1. I will not act like white trash.
2. I will not act like white trash.
3. I will not act like white trash.
4. I will not act like white trash.
5. I will not act like white trash.
6. I will not act like white trash.
7. I will not act like white trash.
8. I will not act like white trash.
9. I will not act like white trash.
10. I will not act like white trash.
11. I will not act like white trash.
12. I will not act like white trash.
13. I will not act like white trash.
14. I will not act like white trash.
15. I will not act like white trash.
16. I will not act like white trash.
17. I will not act like white trash.
18. I will not act like white trash.
19. I will not act like white trash.
20. I will not act like white trash.
21. I will not act like white trash.
22. I will not act like white trash.
23. I will not act like white trash.
24. I will not act like white trash.
25. I will not act like white trash.

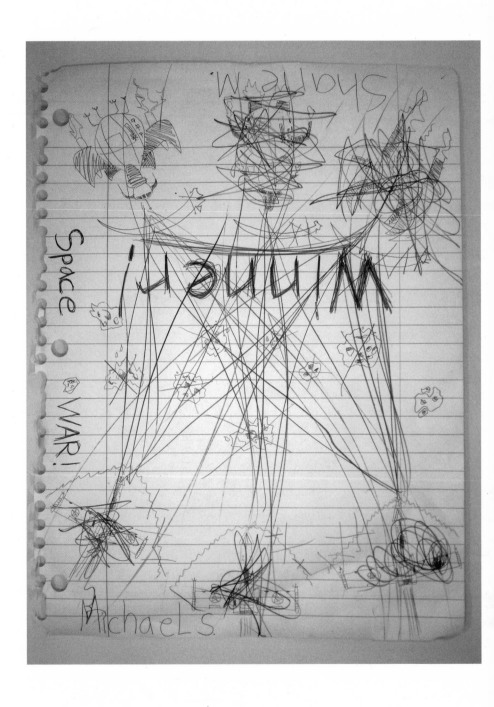

The Ambassador's Daughter

Sarah Borden Wareck

FOR YEARS, WHENEVER TESSA HEARD THE MENTION OF IRAN OR anything Iranian, whether in the context of a name, a new restaurant, or the situation in the Middle East, she remembered a time when she went to school across from Gracie Mansion, when a man with no nose frequented the bus stops of Eighty-sixth Street, and when a gang headed by a pair of redhead twins roamed the Upper East Side. Mostly, she remembered the three months she lived alone with her father over the winter of her fifteenth year. Tessa hated her father then, so she spent as much time as possible out of the apartment, clambering over the banks of dirty snow around the curbs in the grungier downtown neighborhoods, listening to the Psychedelic Furs on her Walkman on the subway, and eating vegetable soup in Greek coffee shops with her friends on cold winter afternoons.

Her parents were getting a divorce and her mother had gone off to a place in Massachusetts—Tessa couldn't figure out whether it was a psychiatric hospital or a spa—to recover from divorce-induced depression. Tessa's mother had left a pile of clean laundry on the guest room bed and the freezer stocked with frozen dinners. Every night at six-thirty, Tessa's father took something out of the freezer and put it in the toaster oven, and then he and Tessa sat across from each other at the kitchen table, which rocked because the floor was sloped a little where it stood.

A month into her mother's absence, during a dinner of defrosted meatloaf, Tessa and her father got into an argument about communism. She was for it and he was against it.

"My teacher says that in a Marxist society, everything is equal," she said. She took a bite of the meatloaf, which was still a little frozen at the center.

"Nothing is ever equal," her father said. "Some people have their health, some don't. Some people are more attractive than others."

Tessa frowned, sensing ridicule. She dropped her fork and put her elbows on the table. Her father's wine jiggled in the glass. "It's just not fair," she said, "that we should have so much without even having to really work for it."

"I work," her father said. He put a chaotic forkful of salad into his mouth. The sound of his chewing dominated the small kitchen.

Tessa fixed his bowed forehead with a hostile stare. She recalled the night before her mother's departure; her mother had taken her out to dinner at the pizza place around the corner, one of the many original Ray's. The redhead twins and their gang were eating at a booth in the back, but because she was with her mother, Tessa felt safe. Her mother pressed a white napkin into the grease of her own and Tessa's slice. "But why do you have to get a divorce?" Tessa asked. "I don't understand why you can't just stay together." The truth was, the thought of her parents together—sleeping together, talking together in their room—was uncomfortable. But she'd gone to some lengths to accept the notion. To have the situation altered now was maddening, as if some tacit agreement among the three of them had been violated.

Her mother sighed and shook red pepper onto her slice. "Your father is impossible to live with," she said.

"What do you mean?"

"Well." Her mother folded the slice in half. "For one thing, I've asked him a thousand times to use a newspaper when he cuts his toenails, but lo and behold, there they are every few weeks on the side of the sink." Tessa had seen them herself; yellow half moons on the prissy white porcelain lip. "He never lifts a finger to help with the dishes. And do you want to know something else? When you were a baby, he never once changed your diaper. I know he's squeamish about that sort of thing, but still. Not once."

This had not surprised Tessa. She had never been close to her father, at least not physically close, though they had connected when she was younger over certain things: the *Oz* books, their mutual love of holidays, a game in which he would pretend to eat her elbows and knees. When she was a little girl of five or six, Tessa would put on a flowing purple skirt with a ruffle at the bottom and dance to a record of Indian flute music. Her father would clap and yell, "Brava!" But her mother had inhabited the undeniable space between Tessa and her father; a space, Tessa felt, where her physical self should have been. Always, when she was tired, sick, hungry, or constipated, she went silently to her mother, as if shielding her father from the secret of her body, something that clearly frightened him. Tessa used to enjoy using her parents' bathroom because it was bigger and warmer than hers. It had a deep, curved bathtub with clawed feet. But a few years ago, she'd overheard her father asking her mother to ask her to use her own bathroom. "She's getting too old for ours," he'd said.

And now he was cutting the frozen meatloaf away from the thawed part with vigorous concentration, as if the fact that he'd driven Tessa's mother away did not bother him at all. "But other people have to work so much harder for less money," Tessa said. She moved her elbows so that the table shook a little more. "Everyone should be paid the same. Everyone should live in the same kind of apartment." Her chest tightened. She reached for her inhaler.

"But if everyone was paid the same for every job, there would be no need for people to improve themselves. Most people wouldn't bother to read or get an education. Not without some sort of incentive." He put a steadying hand on the table and sipped his wine.

The argument ended with her leaving the table in tears. She went to her room and closed the door, and he stood outside and knocked and she shrieked, "Go away! Go away!" She banged her head against the wall. She bit down with all her strength on the wooden bedpost.

She stopped speaking to him except when absolutely necessary. The mornings were awkward; they moved around each other as they got ready for school and work, Tessa pouring milk into cereal, her father pouring black coffee into a cracked ceramic cup. They took the elevator down in silence and parted ways under the building's green awning. It was easier to avoid him on the weekends. Tessa and her friends shopped during the days and then went to a dance or the movies at night. They'd find a flight of brownstone steps and gather there and drink liquor out of spice bottles, huddled up in their mannish thrift store overcoats. The combination of youth and hard liquor and extreme cold was irresistibly joyous; sometimes they spun with their arms out on the salted sidewalk and fell in heaps to the pavement, and older people walking by had to step over them and around them. Wherever they were going they always ran, whether they were in a hurry or not.

Tessa's father ran out of things to defrost and started ordering in. She picked at her food, listening to her father chew and thinking of her mother in the country somewhere, wandering sedated through deep snow.

Then one night, after her father had finished his lo mein and laid down his fork and knife, he looked at Tessa with a terrible red color in his face and said, "You don't know how lucky you are."

That afternoon he'd gotten some news regarding a friend of a friend of his. The friend's friend worked with the American embassy in Iran and lived with his wife and his daughter, who was exactly Tessa's age, in one of the embassy houses. Attached to the house was an indoor pool where the daughter liked to swim after school. The other day the Iranian police had passed the house and seen her through the glass. They arrested her for wearing a bathing suit; they brought her down to police headquarters and sentenced her to forty lashes with an iron whip.

Before her father could intervene, the sentence was initiated. She died on the thirteenth lash.

Tessa's father stared at her, his eyes bulging from his head. She looked back down at her plate. Blood rushed to her cheeks; she felt as if she should apologize, although she'd done nothing wrong. The story had nothing to do with her; yet clearly he meant something by it. She shook her head. "Why did her father have to take her there?" she asked. "Why couldn't they just have stayed here in America?"

"Sometimes people have to do things," her father said. "That's the way the world works."

Years later, Tessa would read in a fashion magazine that because it was illegal in Iran to execute a virgin, young girls sentenced to death were systematically raped. She would spend isolated hours—while waiting for a train, spacing out before the television—reviewing the situation in her head; had they meant the lashes as a death sentence, or had the girl's death been an accident? Would she have been raped anyway, just in case? Or maybe she hadn't been a virgin. But if not, she wouldn't have known to tell that to the Iranian authorities. She wouldn't have known about that particular policy, and if she had she might have known she could get killed for sexual activity alone. And she probably didn't know—hopefully not—that she was going to die. She probably had no idea how much trouble she was in until it was actually happening.

Tessa's father was called to Boston for meetings and Tessa arranged to sleep at a friend's. He dropped her off at school on his way to the airport. He handed her a piece of paper with his numbers on it, which she crumpled and tossed into the nearest garbage can as soon as the cab pulled away.

At three o' clock, Tessa and Shaw ran home to Shaw's building on East Seventy-eighth Street, jumping up to touch the awnings with their fingers and palms. Tessa's chest felt tight and a headache had started behind her eyes. More than once she had to stop and use her inhaler. Her asthma had developed several years ago but since she'd started smoking it had gotten a lot worse. Now she carried the inhaler with her all the time. At Shaw's, she took aspirin and made herself some tea and then the two of them went into Shaw's bedroom and looked at music magazines. On the cover of one was a picture of Billy Idol in a tight black leather jockstrap. She and Shaw kissed the area between his legs, and then they drummed their legs up and down on Shaw's bed and shrieked, "Balls! Balls! Balls!" They heard Mrs. Howard come home and they pulled each other off of the bed onto the floor where they lay giggling and grabbing each other, almost hoping Mrs. Howard had heard them. But when she poked her head into the room she gave no indication that she had. "I picked up a movie for you girls," she said.

At seven o' clock they sat at the dining room table with Mr. and Mrs. Howard, who seemed youthful and fun-loving in a way that Tessa's parents weren't. Mr. Howard had a slightly effeminate Boston drawl and he teased Tessa and Shaw constantly about boys. Mrs. Howard was dark haired and always smelled of jasmine. Sometimes Tessa would see Mrs. Howard sitting on Mr. Howard's lap, or slow-dancing with him as they had cocktails in the living room and waited for her and Shaw to go out. Mr. Howard would always tell Shaw how lovely she looked—this was the word he used—and kiss her on the top of her head. It made Shaw seem innocent in a way that Tessa didn't feel, although not because of anything she'd done. The fact that Shaw's physical feminine self could be talked about, commented on positively even by her father, made this physical self about something besides sex; it was about that too, but mainly it was about her being lovable.

They ate hamburgers with chopped onion on toasted slices of Pepperidge Farm white bread. They ate salad with olives and tomatoes and chopped hard-boiled eggs. Tessa had an acute sensation of missing her mother. She thought of her father in a conference room at a huge table surrounded by men in identical suits. After dinner Mrs. Howard gave them bowls of ice cream and they watched a Marilyn Monroe movie. The ice cream soothed the heated sensation at the back of Tessa's throat. They changed into pajamas and brushed their teeth and got into bed and looked through some more magazines, and at ten Mrs. Howard came in and said, "Lights out in twenty minutes." They heard her walk back into the living room.

"There's a party," Shaw said. "Some Marymount girl."

At midnight they rose from their beds and turned on one light and dressed silently. They sprayed their hair and applied makeup, not daring to wash their hands after for fear the sound of water running would wake the Howards. On their tiptoes they ran to the elevator and pushed each other in. The night doorman let them out, carefully averting his eyes from theirs.

The streetlights were on and the delis and coffee shops were open, but the regular stores and most of the restaurants were closed. The ordinary industrious people in their suits and sneakers were at home in bed, and the faces she glanced into as they walked north looked younger and fiercer. A man with a narrow face and a sharp blue Mohawk; she'd seen them downtown when she went with her friends to the thrift stores, but in the dark it looked like a weapon. A girl with white blonde hair and chewed and bloody lips. A group of heavy metal guys made up in eyeliner and lipstick, their hair long and puffy, their pants tight at the crotch.

When they saw the bright cheery lights of Baskin Robbins they started to run. Their friends were waiting inside, sharing a small sundae. The Marymount party had been cancelled, Thea said, so the girls wandered down Eighty-sixth Street, passing around a spice bottle of gin. They went into a coffee shop and ordered coffee and smoked. Tessa smoked too, although her lungs felt asthmatic and tight. They asked for the check when the noseless man came in and sat in the booth across from them. They wandered again, looking into windows. Tessa saw a woman cross a room holding a baby, a shirtless man peering into a refrigerator, a couple huddled on a couch, their television a faint shifting light.

In one of the basement apartments a party was taking place. The girls looked at each other.

"We could crash," Mimi said.

They stared in through the grimy window. The small room was very crowded. A bar was set up on a card table. A skinny girl in leather pants laughed so that all her teeth showed. A guy with big hair and acne sat with his legs apart and rolled a joint on one knee.

Thea said, "There's this place my brother used to go."

The wooden sign above the door said McCann's, in Celtic lettering. As they walked in they arranged their faces in ways they hoped made them appear older, but no one seemed to notice them anyway. They found a table at the back. Shaw and Thea went to the bar and returned with whiskey sours (what Mr. Howard drank), each girl holding two. They drew their chairs in closely and drank their drinks and waited for something to happen. The room smelled of beer and urine and nicotine. Tiny colored lights wreathed the ceiling and the jukebox played "When Doves Cry." It was two o' clock in the morning. Tessa had the feeling that she had stepped into a vivid, communal dream.

Thea said, "Isn't this song from like, two years ago?"

The door opened and two college-age guys walked into the bar, letting in a rush of cold air. They bought drinks and a pack of cigarettes. They sat at a table near where the girls were sitting and when they saw the girls looking they looked back, and the girls turned to each other, ducking their heads and beginning to giggle.

The guys pulled their chairs over to the girls' table. They asked the girls their names and their ages, which they lied about. They bought another round of whiskey sours. They told the girls their names but Tessa wasn't listening; she was studying their hair—short and spiked up with gel—and their clothes—black pants, combat boots, plaid flannel shirts. The skin on their faces seemed dirty and prickly and rash-ridden but they wore the same thrift store overcoats the girls did and Tessa recognized the name of the high school they said they'd gone to. One of them seemed to have a British accent. He was slight and wore a row of rings up his left ear.

He turned to her and asked, "What kind of music do you like?"

She listed the names of her five favorite bands. He nodded, and added a couple of names.

"Do you want to go to a party?" he asked her.

The accent was fake, she decided. She glanced at his friend. "Is he going too?"

"I guess so."

"Can my friends come?"

"Sure. They can come."

"Where is it?"

"Across town. Near where I live. Near Columbia."

"Do you go to school there?"

"I transferred this year from Michigan. I wanted to be closer to my mom. She's sick." He looked away.

"I'm sorry," she said.

"It's not your fault." He looked right at her, then down at her hands on the table. "You have cute little hands," he said. He picked one of them up and held it in both of his.

He hailed a cab outside the bar. They got out on Columbus and walked up a side street. "This is my block," he said. "I need my I.D. for the party." She looked up at him; he had beautiful, long eyelashes. They climbed a short flight of steps and he unlocked the door to a building, which was squeezed in between two other newer-looking buildings. The lobby floor consisted of small, discolored tiles pieced together at haphazard angles, but the space smelled good, like someone in one of the apartments was cooking something. They walked up two flights of stairs and down a couple of hallways, turning and turning between two pressed-together walls. The walls were painted a brownish orange and the paint was peeling like a scab.

They turned the last corner. He opened a door and flipped the light switch. The room was clean and neat. There was a window seat with the radiator underneath like in her room at home. A white paper shade was raised halfway. "I've gotta piss." He raised his hand in a gesture of hospitality. "Be right back. Make yourself comfortable."

She walked around the room looking at his things. On top of a neat stack of *Rolling Stones* by his bed were an ashtray and a half-full cup of coffee. Loose papers and pencils with the erasers chewed off lay about his desk. Above the desk a bulletin board displayed course schedules, phone numbers, ticket stubs, and photographs: a pretty brown-haired girl smiling, the Clash. She picked up *On the Road* and flipped through it. She went to the window. It overlooked a space between that building and several others. At the bottom of the space was a rectangular pool surrounded by a sort of metal gate, lit from within by a greenish luminescent light. She recalled the indoor pool at her parents' tennis club on East Fifty-second Street, and how she always used to have her birthday parties there, how her mother would make her a cake in the shape of a castle with upside down ice cream cones for the turrets and a moat of silver dragées. Then she thought of the girl in Iran, swimming in the afternoon, and she turned quickly away from the window.

Her eyes watered. Her chest made a small rattling sound. She used her inhaler; her lungs twitched weakly under the intake of mist. The door opened, and the guy re-entered the room.

"What is this?" She tapped on the window.

He stood beside her and looked through the glass. She felt the warmth of his body through his flannel shirt. "Beats me."

"Let's find out."

"What, go down there?"

She stepped away from him. "Come on," she said.

They took the stairs to the basement and went out the back of the building where the trash was kept, up a low cement ramp, across a small open lot. The packed snow creaked under their shoes. The pool glowed green behind the iron gate. The guy boosted Tessa up, making a step with his hands, and she dropped to the other side and waited while he pulled himself over. Cracked islands of pale ice floated on the surface of the water. The lights came from inside the pool, narrow beams shining up from underneath; at the surface, illuminated cloudy tunnels of water merged into a phosphorescent nucleus. She knelt and leaned over. She could see her reflection in the dark water at the edge, her face looked blurry and beautiful. She stuck her hand in and swirled it around. The cold between her fingers made her head hurt.

"You're going to get frostbite or something."

"It's so cold," she said. "It feels good. When I was little I used to dump cold water over my head in the bathtub. I had this orange bucket and I'd fill it with freezing cold water and just dump it over my head. It felt amazing." The cold crept up her arm. "The water in our building gets all hot and cold at the wrong times. Once when my mother was taking a shower the water changed and she got scalded. She had second-degree burns. She had to go to the hospital and everything."

"My mother has cancer," he said. He crouched beside Tessa. They looked at each other in the water. She stared until her eyes began to cross. He drew his finger through her reflected face, breaking it up, making ripples across her mouth and nose. She sat back on her knees, feeling dizzy. She used her inhaler. The protective cap had come off and she inhaled bits of tobacco and candy and lint along with the dose.

"You okay?" he said, and she nodded, though she wasn't sure. He put his hand on her cheek. She stood, moving away from it. She held her nose and jumped.

The water punched her right in the chest and she stopped breathing. She kicked and grasped at a chunk of ice. He leaned over and put his arms under her shoulders and hauled her out.

He plugged in the space heater and gave her the Army blanket. She took off her wet things and wrapped herself up. He sat next to her on the bed and rubbed her bare shoulders underneath the blanket. He tapped her nose and opened his mouth over hers. He said her name—she was surprised that he remembered it. He pushed her down and lay on top of her. She watched the shadow of his eyelashes against his cheek. The space heater whirred. In the next room, someone whistled and dragged a piece of furniture across the floor. His mouth sucked at a patch of skin on her neck and she jerked away— she didn't want a hickey.

"We should go," she said. "My friends."

He opened his eyes. They seemed heavy and drugged. "What?"

There wasn't any party, she suddenly knew.

"I'm hot," she said. She tried to sit up but he pressed her down with his body. He rummaged under the blanket and found her crotch. She shoved at his shoulders with both hands. "I need to use my inhaler." She stood, clutching the blanket around her body, and looked for the inhaler in the pocket of her coat. She looked in the other pocket, then in her wet pile of clothes.

"You don't sound good," he said. He lay on his back on the bed, his arms crossed behind his neck.

"I can't find my inhaler."

"Do you want some tea or something?"

She shook her head no.

"I have a hot pot right here in the room."

"No. No thank you."

"Think you dropped it?" He got up. "I'll go look." He left the room. Tessa knelt beside the bed and touched her forehead against the edge and coughed, her chest muscles aching. He was back in minutes. "Nope. Sorry."

"I want to go back to the bar."

"It's after four."

"Take me home, then." She sucked in a thin slice of air, let it out, and worked for another one. "I need to go home."

He held his arm lightly around her shoulders as he hailed a cab on Columbus Avenue. There were the faintest traces of light in the sky as the cab pulled up in front of her building. She felt grateful, almost like she loved him, but the panic in her body wouldn't let her look at him as she got out of the cab.

She dropped her overcoat on the hallway floor and searched the counter for her father's numbers. Then she remembered the garbage can on East End Avenue. She made some coffee and drank it black. She took a hot shower and tried to breathe in the steam, then put on a nightgown and lay across her bed.

She heard the busy noises of a key in the front door. The creak as the door swung open, then footsteps, the footsteps pausing; her father's voice, "Tessa?"

They took a cab to Lenox Hospital on East Seventy-seventh Street. Her father seemed to know not to ask any questions; that talking would only make the breathless, panicky feeling worse. They went quickly through the emergency waiting area and into a room with an examining table and a machine that, when the nurse turned it on, began to spew a thick, white, dreamlike mist. A mouthpiece connecting to the machine was put over Tessa's face, and she breathed the mist into her lungs. The doctor, a youngish woman with tortoise shell glasses and painted fingernails, asked Tessa some questions. The doctor mentioned pneumonia and Tessa's father nodded. He still wore his business suit; he stood at the end of the examining table, looking back and forth from Tessa to the doctor as if following a tennis match. Tessa was brought to a different room and given a shot of something, and she fell into a black sudden sleep.

When she woke the room was dark, the blinds drawn so that she couldn't see if it were day or night. She sat up. Her stomach dropped. She ran to the small bathroom and grabbed the metal rail around the toilet. She fell to her knees and vomited. Her bowels loosened and before she could get up she'd soiled herself, the watery filth rushing past her inconsequential underwear. Her legs trembled. She wiped them with a towel and stepped out of the mess. She slept again, the same knockout black sleep. She woke and heard her father. He was talking to one of the nurses in a low, concerned voice.

"Not my problem," said the nurse. "She's your kid. Clean it up yourself."

Tessa lay still until she became aware of soft movement in the room, a light somewhere. She opened her eyes and turned in the direction of the light. She saw the bathroom door open, her father kneeling with his back to her. His jacket off, his sleeves rolled up. The fluorescent bulb reflecting off the scalp at the center of his thinning hair. A bucket by his side. He was mopping, his right arm out, and his back made gentle circular movements—which, along with the soft swishing of water, caused her after a short while to drift back to sleep.

Three days later, Tessa waited outside the hospital doors as her father stood at the curb, looking for a cab. It was balmier than it had been in months; sun glinted off oily little puddles of melting snow, dogs pulled happily at their leashes, people had taken off their jackets and wrapped them around their waists. A man selling hot pretzels from a cart waved at her, and she realized she was starving. She walked up to the cart and bought a pretzel from the man with change from her overcoat pocket and ate it as she waited for the cab.

The driver, a swarthy man with a Middle Eastern name, beamed at her as she climbed across the slick vinyl seat. He pulled out from the curb and headed west. Tessa's father turned to look behind them. He said suddenly, "Did you know you were born in that hospital?"

"No." She shook her head. It had never occurred to her to wonder where she'd been born.

"We took you home in a cab, just like this. You were all bundled up, and your mother held you on her lap and we pointed out all the things on the street that were your firsts; your first dog, your first bicycle, your first bus. And so on." He looked away from her and fell into abrupt silence.

They turned onto Madison and headed uptown with jubilant swiftness. Their wheels made a springy sound on the wet pavement. The

Korean delis had moved their flowers and produce out to the sidewalk. Ice water dripped brilliantly from air conditioners and awnings. The cab paused at a light. A small girl and her mother crossed the street wearing matching Burberry coats. The girl stomped her feet in the slush and the mother picked her up. Tessa leaned her head against the window. She tried to imagine being a baby, seeing everything for the first time, tiny and surrounded by her young, hopeful parents. She could, almost. Hot tears ran down her face—for herself, for her parents and their failed love, and finally for that girl, the ambassador's daughter. Her shoulders shuddered under a sudden weight of gratitude. Her father was right. She *was* lucky. Lights went green all up the avenue and they sped by sunflowers, a skinny boy on a skateboard, an old woman with an angry face under a huge fur hat.

The relatives and friends began to arrive a few at a time just after dinner, if you can call dinner that distracted gulping down of a couple of mouthfuls while straining our ears for noises upstairs. (Longo, page 183)

Composition Field 1

Ben Carlton Turner

I.

Best Friends Forever / BFF

Sunlight fills the yard—
the dead heat of afternoon
throbbing from the leaf—
as the garden wall rises behind
 & bars the advance of the street.

An infinite warm breath
washing over the city—
my telephone ringing (so clean & pure).

Thrones / Fingerbang

The girls stream forth giggling & collect
under the lamplit   one hand cocked on hip
the other a bit of ribbon   twisting into hair.
They pass around a bottle of white wine
& run barefoot through the grass & concrete
of abandoned business parks, darting
in & out   the blank walls of night
but for that hot piece of cigarette, that arc
from hand to mouth   merciless & exact

a lone black cable overhead

                              crrrackling.

OPEN CITY

On the Way to Church / 3 A.M. & Walking with Thee

In a thin black suit
boot-heeled in leather
& my gold watch
loose around my wrist
I go rattling down the pews
calling out your name

a wunnerful old rainbow
        loose in my skull.

Sudafed Blisterpack / Sense Event

Not storm but before. Miles of gray
cloud climbs toward snowblind.
The arm crowds with pain. Halothane
a jetliner over ice sheet & trilobite.

Golgotha some distant idea
a lace of veins   a scribble.

II.

Self-Improvement Course / Smoking & Thinking

Neon slanting sideways in the rain
& the light becomes small. Smaller.
Then exits. The air-conditioner
a box at the window, roaring.

One Kool after another, end to end
& tracing shapes into the itch

of sex smeared across the stomach.
Something on its hind legs. California.
Tic Tac Toe. Funny little tanks
& field marshals squaring off.

I wondered where it would all end.
Here you said, right here, pointing
to your belly & I looked & saw
& you were right. It was drawn:

(bummy fucker-fucking bummer)

A Very Good Time / Dancehall

On 9th Street & Avenue A. Shop girls
on their lunch hour, strolling past
cafes & flower stands, sunlit beneath
the leafy canopy. A lifetime of summer
casts from their gaze, clear & direct.
The whole unknown world, the civilization
of thigh crossing over thigh,
cigarette & coffee held just so, holy accoutrements
in those slight & freckled arms awash in grace.

Later still. Holding a frozen glass of fruit & vodka,
a small pill fizzing away at the rough edges,
everybody smoking & laughing & dancing—

how every cell in this world
shall now poise within its own bright light.

Graffiti Wall / Calling Home

Dale was here
but Dale went
& I stayed
& I am here forever
because I love you.

I read it
& thought of you
& was glad.

Composition Field 2

I.

Longinus / Mountain Song

Longinus coming down the mountain
among the tiny white flowers,
the black flies & the dust & rock scarred
lovingly by the hot sun & him walking, thinking of ice.

How it comes & grows
& makes a place
in the earth when it dies.

& above his head, a distance of miles,
a parallelogram of gulls, black dots
wheeling & cycling through, the collected shape
dissolving reforming dissolving again.

& Longinus there, coming down the mountain
remembering the criminal, his kind face
& how it came to still upon the point of his spear.

The Cyclist

Through the tiled colonnade & fountain
metal corridor & car alarm, skeletal crane

piecing iron to iron, rivet to rivet,
the cyclist made his silvery claim—
Let this passage become a necklace
that strings between the crowded city blocks,
jeweled clusters of neon, asphalt, & glass,
clasped by a stillness but for ragged breath.

& in that stillness find the end behind each promise.
We can no longer ride out, unending & infinite,
all never tire & never die, for the bough is not boundless,
the nature of growth being the building toward the building,
& always toward the break.

We don't know those boys. They aren't even there.
Anymore. Just a bicycle frame, a ghost of white paint
& red plastic flowers that says   someone died here.
Small moments for which we might lay down
our secret grief, clasp our hands & finally say something
that has nothing to do with us, everything to do with us.

(He was a good guy. He was.)

II.

Procession

Never remember how we got there
only how we left. So wrong before
the simple house   our tires

oiling & clicking through rain & leaf
someone weeping down & down
down & down all darkening street.

Ben Carlton Turner

Cynosure / See You at the Hospital

I closed my eyes
to the thrash of the crowd
& the flash of the police light.

I heard the people & their wail
& I heard the police & their bleat
& I stood there on the street corner

& felt our mountain collect
& then rise
as the ice between us grew.

(hewasagoodguyhewashewas)

Soft-Core Porno

With the television at a steady hiss
& the window a green wreck
of water thorn & leaf   information
entered   thin & eel-like   every edge
exact   locking & unlocking   un
til the little door   slid back
the memory   of her   calves
like small ivory throats & so loved there

the known streaking toward the unknown
our gentle people simply getting gentler.

The Peacock (ten minutes in a bird's life)

Barbara Fillon

SHE WAS RUNNING IN SANDALS TOO LARGE FOR HER FEET. HER toes pushed forward and curled over the front edge, holding on like clenched fists. A half-inch of shoe flopped behind her. They were beautiful shoes—a three-inch wooden heel and a thick strip of soft, white, silver-studded leather wrapping across the top of her feet.

Her name was Kate, and she was running after her three-year-old son, who was chasing a peacock. Her husband and her sister-in-law both just looked at her as the boy began to chase after the bird. They watched her quickly disappear past a row of large, shiny magnolia trees, then reappear in the distance to the right of the trees, still running farther and farther away.

"Honey, the boy is running after that animal. Someone should run after him," her husband had said to her. He looked perplexed, and he was the kind of man whose confusion made him angry.

Meanwhile, the sister-in-law was eating a chocolate glazed donut. She was the kind of woman who always packed a snack. It was a hot August day, and the thick chocolate icing had become warm and sticky. She was unaware that one small clump of chocolate once firmly lodged on her pinkie finger had begun to slowly slide down her fat arm toward her ample elbow. She could not eat the donut fast enough, even though she was chewing and swallowing almost as quickly as Kate was running.

By the time half the donut was consumed, Kate had broken into a sweat around her forehead and around her collarbone just underneath the brown cotton, scoop-neck blouse she was wearing. She was also wearing tight, cropped jeans. As her toes gripped her sandals, you could see her slender calves flexing.

"Should a mother really wear shoes like that?" asked the sister-in-law. "I mean, they are not so great for running after a child, and I'm not even going to mention that she doesn't really look her age in them either. That's a whole other story. Seriously, she's going to twist her ankle."

"Can I have a bite of your donut?" asked the husband.

"They don't fit her," his sister said.

"No, they don't," he said.

"I don't like those shoes, but she loves them," he said. "She wears them everywhere, even in the house."

"I always wear sensible shoes. Of course I don't have a child to run after but I've got sensible shoes nonetheless."

"How's that exercise program the doctor recommended going?"

"Well, I'm out here in the park, aren't I?"

"I'm going to buy a drink from the concession stand."

"Please get me a Tab," she said.

As the husband waited in line to purchase his drink he placed his hands flat against his rib cage and inhaled deeply. He squinted in the sun, looking at his wife, a speck in the distance. He thought perhaps he should have followed her, but as soon as the thought entered his mind, it was replaced by a familiar doubt. In the end, he just couldn't tell anymore if he wanted to follow her, or if he only thought he should.

Kate had reached a fountain, which was a metal sculpture of three large catfish whose gigantic mouths squirted water at each other and whose ridiculously long whiskers extended two feet into the air. The child was chasing the peacock around it, water splashing on both of them. He then chased the bird around two weeping willows, inadvertently tracing figure eights with his small feet.

"Honey, dear, don't hurt the peacock," his mother said. She held her hand in the mist of the spraying water, then wiped her hand across her warm forehead.

The boy giggled and waddled after the bird. "I not going to touch it," he said.

She chased her son and the bird around the fountain. She then stopped to stare at the creature. The peacock, she thought, was stunning. She had never seen one up close before. She was fit and could have run around that fountain a hundred times, but the bird's beauty stopped her dead in her high-heeled tracks.

"Mama, it's got eyes all over it. That's why I can't catch it. It sees me sneaking up behind it," the boy shrieked in delight. The peacock was stubborn and didn't particularly want to move at all, but the boy was in the mood for a chase, and the bird could endure its stoic position for only so long as the boy's feet got closer and closer.

Pearly white, violet, green, and blue moved in front of Kate's eyes. The peacock had a regal blue, plump breast and a long, thin neck. Kate suddenly felt great sympathy for roosters and pigeons. Did they know, she wondered, how unlucky and inferior their lot was. She was mesmerized by the length of the peacock's tail and its intricate design. Kate's own mother had once told her that when you see things up close, they become less beautiful. As she stood before the peacock, a smile as big as the catfish's mouth swept across her face. *Mother is wrong*, she thought, a revelation that did not surprise her. She looked in the direction of her husband and his sister, but she could barely make them out. They had become two smudgy dots.

"Those aren't eyes," she said, running up to her son and patting his head. "That, honey, is a pattern, a beautiful design that magically appears on the bird's feathers and makes him very attractive to the lady birds!"

"Don't think so," said the child.

She laughed and stood in front of him, kneeling down and holding his little hands, letting the peacock get away. The boy didn't run off though; he stood still, staring into his mother's large, brown eyes. "Some day," she said, "when you are all grown up, you are going to remember the day your boring mother told you that that bird's tail has no eyes, and that if your mother had only a bit of imagination, she would have gone along with your story, and told you to run, faster, faster, faster, to catch those eyes!"

The boy smiled and bent down so that his hands lay flat on the warm ground, and then jumped up and clapped his hands together above his head. "No! Mom, you're funny," he said, and ran around her to pursue the bird.

She stood up, turning toward the fountain. She walked up to the sculpted fish and sat on the cool, concrete rim, took off her sandals and dipped her tired feet into the cold water. She tried to pick pennies up with her toes and then release them. She wasn't even looking at her son anymore but could tell that he was nearby by the familiar sound of his footfalls and the muffled, rustling sound of the peacock's feathers. She closed her eyes and let her feet roam for coins.

"Those are great-looking shoes," said a man who had walked up to the fountain. He was walking a large brown dog, and he was letting him drink inches away from where her toes were picking up pennies.

"Oh!" she said, surprised. "Thank you." She looked down to see the sandals discarded on the ground beside her, the sun reflecting off the metal studs, the leather creased from frequent use. "They are a size, well really only half a size, too large for me, but I bought them anyway." She looked up at the man. "I'm usually more practical," she said, "but they didn't have my size and I had to have them!"

"And where did that strange bird come from?" the man asked.

"It's a peacock," said the child.

"I know," the man whispered to the mother and smiled down at her.

The dog barked, but the man immediately calmed him down. "Max likes to chase birds and squirrels," he said.

"Apparently my son likes to as well," said Kate, and the man laughed. "There's a zoo nearby. I think that's where the peacock came from."

The dog began to lick the mother's toes, and she jumped a bit at first so the man pulled the dog away, but then she assured him that it was fine. She let Max lick her feet and splash about. The dog's tongue tickled her, making her laugh. The child continued to run in a circle, holding his breath whenever he got close to the bird.

"Careful," she shouted to her son, "remember, the beautiful bird doesn't want to be touched."

The man laughed. "It doesn't want its feathers pulled. That's for sure. I'm John, by the way." He extended his arm to shake her hand.

"Kate," she said, and, as she reached for his hand, she lost her balance and fell into the fountain, her pants sticking to her legs and her hair now a mixture of sweat and cold water.

"I'm so sorry," he said.

"No, no, my fault. I'm so hot and tired, I just lost my. . . ." She stood up and shook her hands in the air. "I just lost my sense of place, I guess." She stepped out of the fountain and tried to put her shoes on. He offered his steady arm. She took it.

"Looks like they fit just fine to me," he said. John looked at her feet. Kate looked at John.

"Do you want to go for a walk?" John said.

"What?"

"Come on. We'll walk the peacock back to the zoo before either the bird or your son collapses in this heat. I don't want to see which one goes first!"

"Yeah, I know what you mean." Kate laughed and shook her head in disbelief at this most unexpected situation. She turned to look back in the direction she came from and then she gently bit her lower lip as if there were something still left to consider. She felt refreshed after her soak in the fountain, and she wanted to go for a walk with her son, the peacock, the dog, and this man; the man who had simply told her that he liked her shoes. "Let's walk this way toward the zoo," she yelled to her son. *It's just a walk*, she thought. *Just walking. People come to a park to walk after all, now don't they?*

The boy chased the bird toward his mother, and, once he'd passed her, she began running after him again, this time in a straight line toward the zoo, away from the park and the fountain. *Just running.* John and Max ran along beside her. It felt good to run, and her feet felt more and more comfortable hitting the ground.

What
Calls
Your
Name

Mark C

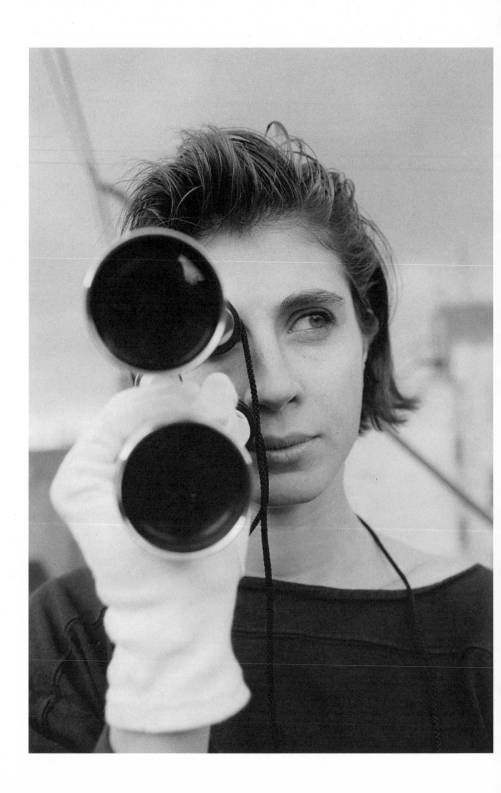

His

apartment was crowded

and dark. The furniture was

too big for a narrow studio. It was the

kind of stuff that was supposed to look

classy, like some middle-class family's notion

of elegance in their living room (with a touch of

hysteria or something)—an elaborate mirrored

cabinet, gigantic stained-glass lamps, the armchair I

was sitting in, and a faux-antique mobile-bar with lots

of bottles. The wallpaper was a dark, boudoir-crimson.

(Ames, page 39)

The Boil

John O'Connor

THAT MORNING IN THE SHOWER I FELT IT: AN ALIEN NUB ON THE underside of my left buttock, just inches from my exit hole on an isthmus of hair that juts into wallet territory. I seized it, taking measure of its girth. When I turned and saw it in the mirror, I shrieked. Staring back at me was a raw pustulant lump, fleshy and pink as a newborn, but with a bulbous head and a translucent, Saturn-like ring.

A boil. An abscess. Whatever you want to call it. A hateful grief pit of pus and blood and dead mucusy tissue that lurks just below the skin's surface and haunts and abuses you like a small-town sheriff at the end of his last term. Boils have been a part of my life for as long as I can remember. Every few months one appears in an earlobe, on my neck, or more often in a well advertised place like the center of my forehead. Some eventually burst and heal on their own. Many more require surgical incision and drainage. In college, a nurse in the student-health services lanced a massive boil in my earlobe, harpooning it with a syringe while her colleague pinned my head to the examination table. Others I've managed to lance myself. Not long after the earlobe extraction and while particularly drunk, I pierced a Cyclopsian boil with a sewing needle, a clumsy procedure that left me with a permanent pea-sized dent just below my hairline. Despite all of this, I tried to stay positive with this ass-boil, telling myself that as

long as I didn't pick it and kept it clean, it would mend itself. I needed
to believe this. It would've been impossible to carry on otherwise. So I
gave the boil a light scrubbing with the loofah, turned off the water,
and tried not to worry about it.

This was during our second month in Senegal, West Africa, as the
rains let up. Giant baobab trees loomed suddenly on the horizon like
an advancing army, with black Griffon vultures perched high in the
defoliated limbs. I was living in Senegal with my girlfriend Stephanie,
a startling, elk-like beauty who I was certain would one day bear my
seed. She had dramatic black eyes, arms and legs that were slender to
the point of emaciated, and long sinewy brown hair that was cut in
the style of the 1990s female tennis starlet Gabriela Sabatini. We'd
known each other for years but never carnally, until the previous
summer in England, where she was studying international develop-
ment and I was dabbling in poverty and alcoholism while intermit-
tently employed as a "barback," which is a kind of chattel slavery with
perks. After a brief, stumbling courtship, we flew into each other like
blindfolded sparrows. My chest acquired new muscle definition. My
brain felt freshly laundered. After three months it seemed perverse to
think of spending a night apart.

Then one day Steph announced she was moving to Senegal, 2,500
miles away, for a new job. This struck me as an ominous develop-
ment. We wept and blubbered together for several nights, mourning
our lost future. I dreamt of a vast wilderness, snakes, awful heat, woke
with hot tears running down my face, and imagined spending the rest
of my life as a sexual hermit. Suddenly she asked me to join her in
Senegal, and unhesitatingly I agreed.

I was twenty-six and astonishingly ignorant about the world. I
imagined life in Senegal as an adventure of unparalleled drama—
perilous safaris, bonfire lunches of grilled wildebeest, cocktails at the
foreign-officer's club. I even packed *The Green Hills of Africa* thinking
Hemingway's bush heroics would inspire me. Unfortunately, as I
soon discovered, there are no wildebeest in Senegal, and the very
notion of a foreign-officer's club expired a century ago. My life there

became less like Hemingway's and more like Clov's in Beckett's *Endgame*; that is, one of almost unrelenting boredom, isolation, and despair.

Steph, who'd done graduate research in Senegal, had warned me to tame my expectations. While not without its charms, Senegal could be a hard place to live, she said. Its location on the edge of the Sahara makes it excessively hot and arid, while its largely Muslim population means two of life's bare essentials—booze and porn—are scarce.

I tried to be realistic. When people asked me what I would do there I'd say something like, "Teach English," which sounded plausible. But the truth was I didn't know the first thing about what that would require and I did zero research. I'd always return to an image I had of myself driving an open jeep through the bush with a rifle slung over my shoulder and antlered game tied to the hood. As I said, I was ignorant about the world.

We lived in a small town called Thiès, amidst a landscape of crumbling highways, gasoline extortionists, and packs of wild dogs. Upon arrival, Thiès looked like a set of an old Western movie, with horses hauling timber carts down wide dusty avenues and ancient, dust-entombed buildings with doors that banged open in the wind. Aside from a few lonely shops and a market that sold bootlegged "Dubacell" batteries and "Nice" tracksuits, the place looked deserted. Actual tumbleweeds rolled through the streets.

After a couple of weeks, the rain that had fallen like artillery fire since our arrival ceased and the midday air acquired a callused, factory thickness. Sweat rolled off of my face into my food. The sky became an endless, blinding thing, so blue it was menacing. Steph, busy at work, was gone most of the day, and I hibernated in the small house we rented, emerging for an occasional sortie to buy Orange Fanta and Laughing Cow cheese. The house sat back from the road a ways and the genius of its design was its slatted windows that permitted a scarcity of light to enter, rendering the house cave-like for much of the day. Its only flaw, we learned, was decrepit plumbing.

The water was sepia-colored and the pipes doubled as a barracks for a Titan race of cockroaches. Our neighborhood also had the distinction of being the only neighborhood in all of Thiès to have its electricity cut off most nights, robbing us of the breeze from our fan.

As some of the only white people, or *toubabs*, around, Steph and I became local celebrities. Each night we received a stream of visitors. Some trekked from across town, culverts of sweat running from them. We dispensed Fanta to these pilgrims and ushered them into porch chairs. Everybody came. Mere acquaintances, strangers. Nobody was turned away. Many wanted only to sit quietly and drink Fanta by the liter. We figured this was how Senegalese socialized. When we wanted them to leave I'd put on some Tom Waits, which for some reason freaked them out.

I couldn't find a job teaching English. There weren't any, and even if there had been I wasn't qualified. My French sounded like a pidgin moon language and I couldn't speak a word of Wolof, the local dialect. As I considered what to do, I went to the movies. There was an air-conditioned theater down the road that specialized in things like *Titanic* and *My Best Friend's Wedding,* plus kickboxing movies and the entire Sandra Bullock catalog, all dubbed in French and rendered watchable only by the small miracle of central-air. In the mornings I'd read under the papaya trees in our backyard, pausing to sip my coffee and marvel at the rising heat, vaguely aware of the pantomime of a colonial provincial I must have presented to our neighbors—a *toubab* lounging on a rattan settee with French opera playing inside. All that was missing was a pith helmet and eyeglass. In the afternoon I'd shoot off to a matinee, crossing my fingers for *Bloodsport* or *Encino Man,* and return home in time for dinner with Steph.

I soon became senseless with boredom. It was clear that unless I found something constructive to do I'd lose my mind. Being low on French, my options were limited, but I found a preschool willing to take me on as a volunteer. For three days a week I worked in a classroom of five- and six-year olds with whom I could barely communicate. At first we just stared at each other, amazed. Later, I taught them how to thumb wrestle. They laughed at my clothes. It was one of those rare symbiotic relationships based entirely on puzzlement and awe. My sole duty in class was to hand out pencils in the morning and collect them at the end of the day, for which I was quietly tolerated by the teacher, a dwarflike Senegalese man in short sleeves and pleated slacks who taught in a listless, melancholic state but who became gripped by demented fury when the kids misbehaved. He carried a weathered yardstick, occasionally slipping it through a belt loop to wear like a sword, which he would unsheathe for a variety of heinous infractions such as whispering. The yardstick would crack like a whip on the kids' palms and buttocks and the classroom would fill with their screaming. They did things differently in Senegal, I was learning.

Despite my obsessive efforts to keep the boil clean, it had doubled in size only a few days after I'd discovered it. I rinsed it constantly with rubbing alcohol and covered it with bandages from my first-aid kit. But the bandages became soaked in sweat, came unstuck, and slid into the crevice of my ass. In another week or so it had calcified into a fleshy knoll about two inches in diameter. It looked like an animated clump of phlegm. Never had a boil ballooned on me so quickly. The pain was scary. My posture became distorted. I ate my meals on the couch with cushions stacked under my leg to keep the weight off the boil. Even this became uncomfortable and I started pacing the length of the house as I ate, clomping through the living room and kitchen and backyard, disfigured and bandy-legged like Quasimodo.

Steph helped me change bandages and clean the boil. Under normal circumstances I would've been reluctant to let her get too close to my bare ass. I'm incredibly hairy down there. Every few weeks I have to hack away the overgrown vegetation in my entire Speedo region or I lose sight of the tree through the forest. I even had to shave a moat around the boil so the bandages would stick to skin instead of hair. But these were desperate times, and I soon realized just how much Steph loved me. It was a gruesome business, not for the squeamish, yet she appeared totally unfazed.

Still, things grew strained between us. A part of me blamed her. I was mad at her for bringing me to Senegal. I wanted to return to London, back to how things were. We'd never fought before, but suddenly we were having apocalyptic arguments in which dishware perished en masse. Nooky was rare. Somehow, joy disappeared from our interactions. Had I not been so despondent or felt so stuck, I might have tried harder, found a different approach. Instead I settled for apathy.

My body continued to fail me. The following week I became terribly constipated. This was induced, in part, by the near roughageless Senegalese diet and exacerbated by the stress and anxiety of my Kilamanjaroan boil. Laxatives were nowhere to be found (the Senegalese are a gastrointestinally resolute people). Coffee wouldn't flush me out. Chronic constipation can tip one dangerously close to the psychic brink, and the digestive blockage and boil together were almost too much for me to bear. The ensuing nine days—a benchmark in human history, I think it's safe to say—were some of the most emotionally harrowing of my life.

I quit going to the school, as much for the physical discomfort it posed as for the small hatred I was developing for the teacher with his yardstick truncheon. At home alone, feeling myself slipping toward a pancreatic shutdown, it began to occur to me that the boil wasn't going to burst on its own and would instead continue to fester and grow at a Blob-like rate, and for the foreseeable future I'd remain stranded in this dusty outpost. Steph pleaded with me to go to the hospital, but we'd been there before when she'd had malarial symptoms, and I refused to pass through its sinister portal again. The place was an abyss of fear and darkness where patients cried out in the halls from their ailments. It'd taken us three visits and countless, fraudulent hours to get her blood drawn and receive the results (it turned out she had typhoid, but fortunately it wasn't serious and she recovered quickly).

Nonetheless, Steph thought I was being a martyr or a coward, or both.

"The hospital is good enough for me and for Senegalese, but not for you?" she asked. She had a point. Maybe the problem wasn't the hospital but the very notion of African medicine. I'd always imagined myself as someone who defied Western cultural prejudices. I mean, I'd read Frantz Fanon and Jean Baudrillard or whoever. But maybe I'm not that kind of person. I didn't want to be heroic or atone for history with this boil. I just wanted it gone. Deep down, I just wanted out of this place.

Several days passed in which I could barely move from my bed. I lay bloated and pale, every horrible movement splintering my ass like cannon shot.

Then one night I awoke to a fierce rumbling in my bowels. I leapt out of bed, a wave of euphoria rushing over me as I sprinted toward the bathroom, and reached the toilet just in time. The effect was like throwing the switch on an electric chair: an incredible amount of juice poured through the system in a matter of seconds, and the ensuing mess was frightening.

My relief was short lived, however, as the boil continued to fester. It had grown steelier and more obscene in its livid, corpse-like pallor. Desperate to be rid of the thing, I decided to try to lance it myself. I stripped naked in our windowless kitchen and poked along the edges of the boil with a sewing needle, wincing and gasping, hoping to perforate its iridescent halo. This achieved little, so I attempted to penetrate the hard morass at the center by jabbing the needle into the top of the boil. But its location on the inside corner of my ass made this difficult. I wrenched my head back as far as I could, craning my neck over my shoulder while steadying myself on the countertop. But I could barely glimpse it this way. Closing my eyes, I swung the pin onto the vicinity of the boil again and again, howling with every thunderbolt. It was like a game of pin-the-tail-on-the-donkey, except that the donkey was me. This went on for a minute or so, until I couldn't bear it any more and crumpled to the linoleum. Straddling a mirror later, I saw that I'd only managed to break the skin's surface in about a half a dozen places and failed to puncture the boil itself, leaving several horrific gashes along the fleshy edges.

Regrettably, I hadn't thought to sterilize the needle beforehand and the boil quickly became infected. By the time Steph returned home that night it had mutated into an evil black welt about the size of the top of a Pringles can. When she came in, I was lying on the couch with my pants around my ankles and an icepack wedged up my ass.

"Ahhh!" she screamed, recoiling in horror.

"What happened?" she asked. I told her. She shook her head. "Bravo," she said, clapping ponderously. "Bravo."

From then on my nights were terrible. I'd roll onto the boil in my sleep, sending tidal shocks through my ass. A frenzy of cursing and moaning would overtake me as I struggled out of bed and limped into the bathroom to splash tepid water on the boil. Returning to bed, my brain would lurch into a kind of tailspin and I'd stand in the hallway whimpering, a wilderness of despair rising around me, my mouth about halfway open to a scream.

One night, about two months into the ordeal, I staggered into a neighborhood grocery store run by a guy named Samuel. Samuel had a quick smile and spoke a simple French uninfected by Wolof that was easy for me to understand. We talked often.

The shop was a converted garage. It was dark and cool with a single lightbulb hanging from the ceiling, which always reminded me of the Dustin Hoffman interrogation scene in *Marathon Man*. Samuel and I chatted on a bench by an open door, watching children playing in the darkening street. It was hotter than usual. My clothes clung to me. As I grimaced at the boil chafing against the bench, Samuel asked what was the matter. I hesitated. There was the low crackle of a radio in the distance. People passed by on the sidewalk, nodding hello, mumbling "*Assalam Alaikum*." Then for some reason I broke down. I told Samuel about the boil, about my sleepless nights, my failed lancing, and even my antipathy toward the local hospital. He leaned back and peered at my ass, his mouth splitting into a huge grin. Straightening, he suggested I go see a griot—a kind of tribal medicine man—who would gladly fix my boil, free of charge.

"A griot would love to get a hold of that thing," he said as laughter seized him and rocked his body back and forth in the twilight. "That's a once in a lifetime opportunity for a griot."

"Har har. Very funny," I said. The momentary relief of my confession gave way to a familiar desperation. As Samuel guffawed and slapped his knee, I wondered aloud whether I might qualify for a Red Cross airlift to New York.

Recovering himself, Samuel told me about a private medical clinic just down the road where a doctor could treat me for a modest fee. Wealthy Senegalese went there. "Don't worry," he added. "They treat *toubabs* too." With these magic words, I relented.

The next morning Steph and I walked to the clinic. It was windy out and we held onto each other while shielding our eyes from the dust. The clinic was just a few blocks away. I must have passed it a hundred times without realizing what it was. Staring at it now, I wondered what horrors it held. The building had recently been painted a pasty, sluggish pink with sky-blue trim, which was probably meant to be cheery but depressed me immensely.

The door was open but the lights inside were off. A few elderly Senegalese men were standing around outside talking. I interrupted to ask if the doctor was in. One of them turned to me, his skin lying in great folds across his face and neck. He wore a long white robe and skullcap and was clutching a knobbed ebony cane. After mumbling something in Wolof, he returned to his conversation. Steph and I looked at each other and shrugged. I tried again, but louder. "Is the doctor in?!" Suddenly the man swung around, shouting and shaking his cane in my face. I held my hands up, worried he might have my skull in his cane's crosshairs. Steph and I were about to retreat when someone emerged from the clinic. He was a Kabila type, round and stocky with fat limbs and black-rimmed glasses that were much too small for his face. He looked me up and down, said something in Wolof to the old man, and then beckoned Steph and I through the door.

Our savior turned out to be the clinic's doctor. His name, which I've forgotten, was written on a nameplate on his desk. The inside of the clinic was painted the same pink with blue trim as the outside. It reeked of disinfectant, which I took as a good sign. Relieved to be free of my nemesis outside, I rambled on to the doctor about my boil. He cut me off to say he had a niece attending college in Minnesota, studying "American policy." He then told me to lie on my stomach on a gurney with my pants down. I obliged. He snapped on a pair of rubber gloves, gently parted my ass with his fingers, and examined my boil through his toy-store spectacles.

After a few seconds he looked up and said, with a hint of melodrama, that I'd come to the right place. He could fix me for the price of twenty Central African Francs, or about thirty U.S. dollars. Steph gave him the money. He scribbled something on a slip of paper, handed it to me, and told us to go upstairs and find a man named Moussa. After some searching, Steph and I found Moussa sitting in a closet cluttered with glass vials and stacks of green towels, picking his cuticles with a long metal poker. He looked remarkably like the former pro basketball player Muggsy Bogues, except that he had a two-inch Afro and was wearing hospital scrubs inside out.

I handed him the slip of paper. He examined it, grinned eerily and then motioned for us to follow him down the hall. My heart pounded. I knew that whatever awaited me, it wouldn't be pretty. We paused at a large room where a dozen or so people were milling around. Moussa told Steph she'd have to wait here. I held her hand until the last second. She whispered, "Jack . . . Jack," like Kate Winslet in *Titanic* as Leo DiCaprio sinks into his icy grave. I chuckled, though inside I was dying.

Moussa led me to yet another pink room with blue trim, where I again had to lay on a gurney with my pants down. A network of shadows and cracked masonry emerged, and a sliver of light from a desk lamp fell across my back. On a tray next to my head were several scalpels and other medical implements, including a giant pair of scissors, hemostats, forceps, piles of gauze, and some metal canisters filled with a clear lubricant. The towel on which all of this was laid was splattered with dried blood, as was the wall in front of me. Again there was the smell of disinfectant. As Moussa slipped on a pair of rubber gloves and began swabbing my boil, the doctor walked in carrying a huge syringe. My lungs emptied. It was so big it looked like a stage prop.

The two of them spoke briefly in Wolof. I wanted to ask about the procedure, but before I could the doctor swung the syringe into the air and brought it swiftly down onto the boil. PLUNK! I screeched. The pain was transcendent. For a moment it seemed disconnected from my body. Then it was upon me fully. I wailed, baring my tonsils. The muscles in my legs contracted, pitching my body sideways, and Moussa leapt onto me. I could feel his strength in my legs as he fought to keep us from spilling off the gurney. Clutching the handrails, I buried my face in a pillow and let loose shrieking animal noises. At some point I began to hear sounds coming from somewhere far off, a muffled heaving followed by short, steady grunts, which I soon recognized as my own.

Almost as quickly as it arrived, the pain subsided. My leg muscles relaxed and Moussa climbed off. I glanced back to see the doctor slowly rotating the needle around in the boil, pausing to allow pus to trickle into the syringe's vial. He smiled and pointed with his free hand while Moussa nodded along. They seemed to be enjoying themselves. For some reason—relief, fear, or exhaustion—I started to sob.

Seeing my distress, the doctor explained what he was doing with the syringe. The rotating, he said, was to extract as much of the pus from the wound as possible and ensure that the infection wouldn't return. I didn't see the effect of this until the bandages were removed a few days later, but the rotating tore a quarter-inch hole in the top of the boil.

The doctor extracted the needle and twirled it like a baton into a trash can. He showed me the vial, clasped between his thumb and forefinger. It was several inches long, about an inch in diameter, and filled with a rosé of blood and pus.

"Look," he said, smiling and patting me on the shoulder. "The two colors, red and yellow."

"Yes, I know, " I said while wiping the slobber from my face. "I've seen them before."

Thinking it was over, I sat up on my elbows and let out an exhalative sigh. Then I noticed Moussa fixing some gauze to a pair of hemostats. The doctor, on his way out the door with the vial, presumably to give it a proper burial, patted me on the shoulder again and said, "You are very brave."

Moussa announced that he needed to disinfect the wound. Before I could brace myself, he inserted the hemostats into the opening. Once more, the pain was surreal. I flailed as he swiveled the hemostats around. A long piercing squeal escaped me that seemed to startle even Moussa. At that moment, with my vocal chords distended and my body in a Superman-in-flight pose, I noticed that in addition to the blood on the wall in front of me there were flecks of blue paint, evidence of a shoddy trim job.

It was all over in a few seconds. Moussa bandaged me up and I limped into the hall with my pants buckled loosely around my waist. I found Steph in the waiting area talking to the doctor. She put her arm around me and said that everyone there had heard me screaming and felt sorry for me. People stared. The doctor walked us to the exit and said goodbye. As he headed back down the hall I thought I heard him mutter to himself, "That was difficult to see."

The old men were still hanging around outside. I tried to rush past them, but my nemesis raised his cane to my chest, stopping me in my tracks. He asked, in French this time, whether I was feeling better. His eyes were kind. The other men smiled. It seemed that they, too, had heard my screams. "I'm fine," I said, mentioning that I had to return tomorrow, as Moussa had said he'd need to clean the boil one more time. The old man closed his eyes and nodded. Placing a hand over his heart, he looked at me and said twice, *"Al-ham-du-Allah,"* or, "Praise be to God." We shook hands. As I turned to leave I caught a glimpse of him out of the corner of my eye. He was smiling broadly and staring at my ass, where under my pants a mountain of gauze and surgical tape covered a quarter-inch hole.

There are no streetlights in Thiés. At night the darkness is complete. The sky fills with bats and smoke from small trash fires. On the night of my ass crucifixion, Steph and I toasted the end of the boil in our courtyard with a bottle of Fanta. I couldn't see her face for the darkness. I stood with my hand on her shoulder, smiling in a narcosis of relief, feeling as though I'd paid all of my bad debts in this lifetime. Steph shifted around on her feet, crunching the sand with her flipflops. Smoke plugged our nostrils. Finally she said, "The worst is over."

I left Thiès about six months later to start graduate school in New York. Steph had another year on her contract so she stayed behind. The last time I saw her was in the Dakar airport as I was waiting to board a flight home. The rims of her eyes were pink. She had a distant, hollow look, as if this was the ending she'd expected all along. When it was time for me to board we hugged and said goodbye. I cried myself down the jet way.

In the seat next to me was a dark-skinned Senegalese man who fidgeted and sweated a lot in a heavy wool tunic. Before takeoff, a flight attendant approached and asked whether we wanted fish or chicken for dinner. The man spoke only Wolof and didn't understand. The flight attendant, an American woman, was instantly exasperated. There were no other Senegalese nearby, so the three of us tried to figure it out ourselves. We were not a good team. I said something like, "Um . . . er . . . uh." Anguish spread across the man's face. The flight attendant sighed. Just as she was about to give up, it came to me. I turned toward the man and started flapping my arms, making the international sign for chicken. He got it. We both ordered the fish. Moments later we were handed cold Cokes. He cracked his open and guzzled it down. When he finished, he turned his palms up and began praying, murmuring in Arabic. I sat back in my seat, thumbing the window shade. Rain splattered the tarmac as we taxied. The engines rumbled, wheezing briefly as if reconsidering our departure, before lifting us, finally, conclusively, into the falling light.

The Fucker

Jon Groebner

UNDER COVER OF NIGHT, AT DAWN'S FIRST GLOW, SWEATING beneath the noonday sun. Drunk. Sober. Ecstatic. In despair. In dimly lit basements. On couches. On hide-a-beds. On waterbeds. On a grassy slope. On the loneliest prairie in Nebraska. On the hood of a Plymouth two-door Fury sedan. By moonlight. By candlelight. By flashlight. Pelted by hailstones. With hookers. With strangers. With cousins. With the wives of friends, and with the wives of clergymen. With his own wife, faithfully, for several nights at a go. In hotels. Also in motels. Once, behind an ice machine. As many times as possible. With whomever was willing. Alone, a thousand times.

Whom

First was a girl, Gertrude. Later, neighbors and coworkers, babysitters, bankers, psychologists, tourists, and wedding photographers. Women met at gas stations. The hatcheck girl in the coatcheck room. Starlets attired in borrowed dresses. His wife's hairstylist, hurriedly, astride the hydraulic swivel chair his wife had sat in minutes earlier as a paying customer, the floor still strewn with snippets of her hair.

Once on a passenger train rattling slowly out of Cheyenne, Wyoming, the fucker eased himself into the wife of Wyoming's governor, a distinguished older lady who preferred railroad travel to life in the governor's mansion, and pinched her own nipples in the throes of passion.

In the back row of a 737, sailing high over the cornfields of Kansas, he penetrated a flaxen-haired college girl, a sophomore at Bryn Mawr who was majoring in religious cataclysm. Her father, she said, was the day manager at the famous South Dakota Corn Palace.

On a New Year's Eve, later in life, he lost his erection inside a former Miss Montana while standing in the women's lavatory of Ernie's E-Z All-Night Lounge, on a dark night in Hoboken, New Jersey. He took his failure quite badly. The former beauty queen tried to cheer him up, back in the lounge, telling him about the indignities of the Miss America Pageant—the Vaseline inside your lips, the two-sided tape, Bob Barker and his fiendishly white teeth—and he pretended to laugh, but inside he was weeping. In the coming days he developed a sore.

The Wherewithal
The fucker held no job for long. He traveled, staying on the move. When he was a boy, his father, who built pianos, was killed—one of the big saw blades hooked the man's sleeve and took the arm off with a merciless zip at the elbow. He died within minutes. On the advice of a bailiff who lived down the street, his mother hired a lawyer, sued the factory, and won. A few weeks later she drove her car into the lake. And a small fortune went to him.

The Technique
All great fuckers will tell you the trick is trying. Your eyes flicker across a room like a crow casting about for a shiny object, seizing on a telltale slouch, a sucked tooth, a spine unnecessarily arched. Excuse me, you say, what do you think of men who wear hats? Or, in another mood: Hello, my name is X. I have just recovered from malaria. I have no wife. The trick, he realized very early in life, was simply to start talking. The topic could be killer bees, Presbyterians, the lonesome life of the postman, what mattered was to keep talking, to look at her,

to listen, to smile when she smiled, to let her know, telepathically, that you'd do anything to please her. Yes, yes, oh yes, yes.

Then comes the moment when you feel like a magician. You've picked your assistant from the audience, and she wants you to cut her in half.

The Reason
It was not because he wanted to have sex with his mother.

First Love
Gertrude. She was fifteen. They met eating ice cream. The fucker was not yet a teenager himself, only twelve years old, walking into a friend's kitchen—and there she was, spooning herself a bowl of Neapolitan ice cream. She leaned in on the scoop, biting her lip with concentration, straining fiercely against the frozen dessert. He could feel the room come into focus. Something in the way she looked up at him, using her thumb to detach his ice cream from the scoop—an act so simple yet so freighted, he knew it was going to happen. She was the friend of somebody's cousin. Hello. Hello. And he found himself, a few hours later, perched on his forearms on top of her in a dark corner of the cousin's musty basement, quaking with excitement, his knees pressing against the cold wet canvas of a WWI Army cot. Slowly, quizzically, the girl guided him in. There, she said. That's it. He lasted no more than four seconds, two thrusts. It felt as though his soul, cracked open by angels, had dipped gently into warm molasses.

The Vessel
Physically, the fucker resembled a secondary figure in a Roman fresco. Even as a boy, he had a large hooked nose. His chin was soft, dimpled. He had a paunch. His hair—shiny and dark—retreated from his forehead as he grew older. When beseeching, he held his hands in front of him, with the palms up, as a penitent might. As if to say: let me touch, let me cradle. From across the room he had the

air of a man unsettled by his desire to sin, by the sight of a woman's lips parting, the sudden white glint of her teeth.

The Wife
Well, that was a mistake.

The Wounds
Resulting from the act itself: the standard chafing. Some chapping. His jaw, depending on the preamble, might ache for hours. His calf muscles cramped. His testicles, even toward the very end of his life, throbbed nightly for release.

From the hands of strangers: A broken nose. A cracked rib. Countless scars. One jilted mistress, hiding behind a hedge, struck him squarely in the shins with a croquet mallet. He was pushed down stairs. He was slapped and scratched. One lover bit him, passionately, until she drew blood. As a boy, kissing Gertrude, he chipped a front tooth.

The Fear
To die too soon. To miss out. To fail. To flop. To want it but not have the courage to ask for it. To grow weak without warning. Life leaks relentlessly away, he knew, and every night in his dreams, an enormous grandfather clock ticked off the seconds, its heavy pendulum swaying to and fro, a long flaccid nightmare penis. The sound of the ticking clock filled the darkest hallway in his soul. One night, a door in the clock opened and a girl scampered out, wearing only panties, covering herself with her arms, and stepping lightly on the balls of her feet so that no one would hear her, no one would wake. Feverishly, for the rest of his life, he gave chase.

An Easy One
A girl on the bus. A love chick. He is in Cleveland, but it could just as easily be Cincinnati, Topeka, or Cheyenne. The girl wears oily jeans and a frilly, nearly see-through blouse—a pale, thin embroidered

thing with a row of small five-pointed red stars across the chest. He has never seen this type of outfit before. He's transfixed.

Are you looking at me? asks the girl.

I am looking at you, he replies.

What for?

I like how you look.

How old are you? she says.

How old do you think?

The girl makes a small display of scrutinizing his jowls, his paunch, his soft hands. He wears a tan suit with modest lapels. He has dressed for a rendezvous with a banker, the woman who manages his account. It's chilly. Even on the bus, the air has a bite.

Thirty-five? she guesses.

Really? The fucker is sixty-two.

Okay, fifty. She smiles.

The bus lurches to a stop and he slides over into the seat next to her. I'm married, she says, flipping aside her inky hair. You should know.

You don't look old enough to be married, he says.

He's very jealous, she says. He'll murder you with a kitchen knife. I'm not kidding. Another smile steals over her face.

Beneath the frilly cotton top, underneath the oily jeans, this girl is nude.

Well, then, he says, we can't let him catch us.

Her apartment is dingy, at the top of five flights. The bed is fusty. It smells of onions, but it doesn't matter. He has her whimpering soon enough, arching her back, grinding into him as if he alone might scratch an unreachable itch. How long have they been squirming, gasping for breath, before her husband materializes in the doorway? A wiry man with ropey arms. An Adam's apple like a jagged rock. He might not even be real. But then there are footsteps in the kitchen, a rattle of dishes. The girl is on her feet, wrapping herself in a sheet.

No time to dress. Only to disentangle. Go. Run. His bare feet slap the stairs. His penis—pale, wet, absurdly stiff—bounces maniacally in front of him as he careens his way down the stairs, into the lobby, onto the street.

The Act Itself

Entering her, whoever she was, was always bliss. Warmly enveloped, his cock all but glowed. He felt lit from within. The fucker could forget all of life's nastiness: his pale, bloodless father; his mother's slow drive into a cold lake; time's clock with its dreaded tick, tick, tick—all of them disappeared like so many elephants behind a conjurer's cape. For the moment, no future. For the moment, no past. Thrusting, he was alive.

And then, inevitably, he came. Or she did. And he withdrew. And always an unbearable emptiness washed over him, and he was sure he would drown in it.

The Last One

A widow, elderly, spry. She had twenty-seven grandchildren, born to her ten daughters—evidence, she remarked, of a sexual tendency. Did he have children? He had often wondered, but there were none that he knew of. That was lucky. He would have been a disappointing father. The widow patted his arm. Don't think of it, she said. It's not for everyone. Her late husband, she went on, pointing across the room, died in his La-Z-Boy chair. Bless his soul. He yanked the lever back, and shot on through.

The fucker held her. Even after so many encounters, his hands still trembled. The widow's skin felt papery, deliciously soft. He would go slowly. Outside it was autumn, sunny and crisp. Early afternoon. All the time in the world. He was already semi-erect as she fumbled with the buttons of his trousers.

I want to hold it, she said.

There followed a peculiar handshake. Then, without letting go, she led him off to an enormous bed the size of a castaway's raft. I've always enjoyed a nice prick, she said, increasing her grip. Such an optimistic instrument.

Gently, he whispered.

Oh, honey, she said. I know you like it.

As they slide into the cold sheets, Gertrude joined them—a flash across the fucker's mind. He could hear her quick breathing. The little moan she made. How delicately she had coaxed him in, how excited he'd been. It was so long ago. It had lasted only seconds. And then it was never over. To be a little boy, he thought, and to have no idea!

He was aware of the widow wiggling beneath him. But inexplicably he smelled grass. He tasted mints. Pain spread like ink across his chest. Please, he thought, before he realized he was dying—when he thought he was only coming—not yet. Not yet.

The combination
of youth and hard
liquor and extreme
cold was irre-
sistibly joyous;
sometimes they
spun with their
arms out on the
salted sidewalk and
fell in heaps to the
pavement, and
older people walk-
ing by had to step
over them and
around them.
Wherever they
were going they
always ran,
whether they were
in a hurry or not.
(Wareck, page 107)

Drawings

Duncan Hannah

Jon Adrian NYC   DH 05

Stones

Howard Altmann

I would like to be a stone.
By the side of a road.
On a roadless island.
Of no interest to man.
Of no curiosity to animals.
Invisible to birds.

I would like to step out of my stone.
And be another stone.
On the other side of the road.
Prized by man.
Of solace to animals.
A spot for birds.

And on my stone
both stones, please.

Gymnast in the Dark

Something is wrong and you don't know what it is.
The ladder to your thoughts is where you left it.
The inventory of your feelings is catalogued and stacked.
The rooftops which log your horizon at night
Billow the same smoke at morning.
Socks are in the drawer.
The bed is made.

Something is wrong and you don't know what it is.
Memories travel the same tunnel to reach you.
Voices find the same bridge to cross your empty space.
The people you know do not change
What you know about yourself.
Your shadows capture your weight.
The sun does not discriminate.

Something is wrong and you don't know what it is.
You enter every room.
You exit empty-handed.
You ask the silence to invert itself
Like a gymnast in the dark.
Your mind and your heart are one.
The body does not lie.

Howard Altmann

Something is wrong and you don't know what it is.
Light after light and you keep walking.
You turn corners and square your breath.
Night weighs the sky
As oceans scale the rain.
You are part of the universe.
The universe is at sea.

Island

The moment one says it is a moment
of perfection, it is something less
than perfection. So on the island
of Fernando de Noronha, I will be quiet
now. I will let the birds speak
Portuguese. I will let the waters speak
dialects of green. I will let the rocks
tell me I was never really born;
and the vistas carry my insights
to an early death. I will let the breeze
nudge my years off one cliff here
and one cliff there. I will let the air
confiscate my passport. And I will let
the sand send my battles to the sea.
Let them all simply make an island
out of me. The moment I say I am lost
without love, I will be something less
than lost.

Howard Altmann

Sunday Monday

Now you know everything.
I opened the window
And all my air
Fell off the ledge
Into your chest.
You turned it over
In your bed of thoughts
And combed through it
For something to keep.
You kept these words.
To yourself.
And returned to my door.
We stood at the window.
We sat out the silence
With silence.
We watched Sunday leave.

We

swore

to

keep

in

touch,

the

contemporary

West

Coast

vow

of

enduring

passion.

(Stone, page 1)

Conjectures about Hell

Giuseppe O. Longo
Translated from the Italian by James B. Michels

I WANT TO TELL YOU ABOUT THAT NIGHT, BECAUSE BY DOING SO maybe I will be able to escape this whirl in my head and put a little order into these memories that rush out from everywhere and swell among mute and bewildering colonnades that start up again and again just when everything seems to have stopped.

The relatives and friends began to arrive a few at a time just after dinner, if you can call dinner that distracted gulping down of a couple of mouthfuls while straining our ears for noises upstairs. The doctor had been there since morning, even if his presence, as he made a point of telling us, was now superfluous. "But I am doing it out of friendship." Old Galileo wanted us to put him in the big chair in a corner of the dining room where he could see both the living room and the first flight of stairs. The two old women looked at each other and giggled while they helped him sink into the cushion with the torn cover. Toward eleven the house was full of people and upon arriving everyone went upstairs for a moment to see the aunt, then they came back down shaking their heads and glancing at me askance. Then they immediately took the arm of someone they hadn't seen in a long time and struck up conversations.

Old Ersilia went back and forth between the dining and living rooms with the tray full of steaming little cups. "Have some coffee, it will do you good," and hands reached out to help themselves managing the sugar and the little spoons. From his big chair Galileo looked around him with his washed out eyes searching faces for a ledge to cling to. Unstable little groups formed and dispersed beneath the glowing chandeliers, some changed groups to say and hear the same things, so that it actually seemed that at that particular hour nothing could be really new. Whoever sat immediately felt their position too precarious and began again to move about the room. I went into the big kitchen where the two old women were busy making sandwiches, bickering in low voices. Their shapeless backs were turned toward me and they were hissing over which of them was in charge tonight. When I came in they nudged each other with their elbows and turned toward me, smiling from their black mouths. "They will be ready in a minute, take one in the meantime, you mustn't lose heart." Mechanically I chose the biggest sandwich, the salami glistened and left a greasy stain on the tray. It was getting cooler and through the open window a stream of air scented with the night came in from the garden. Someone was walking on the little path outside, stirring up the gravel. I could tell Ferdinando's voice: "I didn't recognize him, he's aged. When I saw him, just imagine, I introduced myself." The steps faded into the rustle of the branches. Over my shoulder the two old women had begun to whisper again and were arguing over the tray of sandwiches. Ersilia came in and said they were hungry out there, the old women stepped up their efforts and went out sideways, bumping into the doorframe. All of a sudden the kitchen was silent, from the living room came the hum of all the people who had invaded the house, then the exclamations at the arrival of the sandwiches.

The doctor appeared, made a half-smile and gave me a conscious look, but really there was nothing to add. Giorgio and Tommaso came to tell me that Enrichetta had been feeling poorly and wanted to see me, the doctor said: "It will be better if I come too." In the living room, the groups had changed completely, someone went out into the garden, through the open door came gusts of tepid air and the chirpings of crickets. Enrichetta was half-lying on a small armchair and old Ersilia was fanning her withered face: "Take heart, Miss Enrichetta, you must be strong." Ferdinando came in again, but seeing his sister in such a state of collapse, he immediately lowered his voice. "This is nothing," said the doctor with an air of certainty and to demonstrate, he looked everyone in the eye, then took her pulse. Gradually the groups arranged themselves around her and Enrichetta said she needed air. Everyone held their breath, some put out their cigarettes, then in the silence a trailing lament came from upstairs. We looked up and abandoned Enrichetta, who had opened her eyes wide and said: "God, God, here it comes." The quickest were the two old women who went into the corridor pulling on each other's blouses and running as fast as they could in their slippers. I went immediately after them and saw that Antonio, Leandro, and Orazio were following me up the dim staircase. Above, all the windows were closed, the aunt was stretched out on the newly made bed and was breathing regularly but with difficulty. The nurse, huge in her white blouse, was seated on the edge of her chair and looked at us severely. I felt embarrassed because all was quiet and there was no reason to have come up here behind the two old women who were now huddling together in a corner and looking at the dying woman with shining, almost frightened eyes. Shaded toward the bed, the lamp cast our long shadows to the ceiling. We tiptoed down again and Ersilia announced that there was some grappa, if someone wanted a little reinforcement. Ferdinando had taken Enrichetta by the shoulders and was walking her up and down the room with her stiff legs and falling bosom. Beneath her blouse you could see the protrusions of corset stiffeners and shoulder straps, so that it looked like a sack of cords and strings. Many had begun to smoke again and were passing around the grappa. Galileo was fumbling around with trembling hands in one of his pants' pockets, his head dangling on his chest. The two old women came down too, saying: "The poor thing, it's obvious that she is suffering," and then they shushed each other and disappeared into the kitchen.

I went out into the garden while Italo was saying: "If it doesn't rain soon the harvest will go to the dogs," but the sky was starry and there was a sultry mist in the breeze. In the dark I recognized Gianna's white dress and I went up to her. She turned without speaking and fixed me with big eyes in a pallid face. Voices and kitchen noises were coming from the house. I felt completely disoriented as if in just that moment I had emerged into consciousness and understood that I existed, transitory and adult. That was my life, those precious and fleeting things, Gianna's face in the summer night, her breathing, the sounds around me: nothing was deferred, everything was consummated then and there. In the lower part of the house the windows were all lit up and you could see the people walking and changing places, moving from one group to another. Through the open door I saw Enrichetta, who walked clinging to her brother's arm, flinging her legs out here and there, one step after another. Above, only the aunt's window was lit, a faint and quiet light. The wind passed through the cypress, it came down upon us from invisible skies, Gianna's dress fluttered, her hair stirred. In that night that never ended, I could have told her faraway things, given a meaning to my life in one prolonged act of adoration, without thinking of afterward, of the rest of my days and years. Behind us someone walked over the gravel but we were so still that our union was impenetrable. I would have liked Gianna to rest her cheek on my shoulder to tell me she understood my dismay or at least to stay and gaze with me at that invisible point beyond the night. It was like going up onto a steep bridge with a vast landscape revolving around us and an immense abyss below. In the house there was bustling and shadows stirred, we ran too behind the others and thronged up the stairs. Above, we all slipped into our places as if by tacit agreement, the two old women elbowed each other for the front position. Squashed between the bed and the wall, the nurse bent over our gasping aunt and looked into her face. I saw the heads, the shoulders of the relatives and acquaintances, the furrowed brows, the glistening skulls, the wide eyes, Enrichetta was crying quietly and Galileo's voice could be heard from below: "What's happening? What's happening?" After a while, over-coming the inertia of the group, the doctor made his way through and said: "You are cutting off her air with this heat," but no one moved. It was only when the nurse stood up and looked severely around that we began to leave, and Ersilia asked me in a low voice if she should make more coffee. Downstairs, in slow coagulations, the groups re-formed and everyone began smoking again between the living room and the garden.

All stooped over, Enrichetta was saying to Gianna that she felt sick because the thought of our aunt dying tormented her. "She must be suffering so much, poor thing." "No, no," said Antonio who was mov-ing from one group to another, "she is feeling nothing, it is we who are suffering," and Orazio nodded while drinking his coffee. The two old women gathered up the empty little cups and the ashtrays, some-one asked me if I intended to sell the house. "I don't know, I haven't thought about it," and I was looking at old Galileo, at the trembling of his gnarled hands. I went back into the garden and over to the hedge where a little earlier I had stood with Gianna and within myself I invoked her, please come help me. Instead Tommaso and the doc-tor came over. "You shouldn't smoke if you suffer from asthma." From the house the grandfather clock tolled two and as if they had been waiting for that signal everyone began coming out, walking over the gravel and shifting the iron chairs. The dog howled briefly. "Oreste wrote to me the other day, he says he's getting married soon. She is French," said Italo. The window above was still closed and weakly lit, on the other side behind the trees there was a kind of radi-ance, but dawn was still far off. A train whistled in the countryside and its sound widened with the wind into the night. I went back in, avoided Galileo's tearful eyes and went up to my aunt's room. The nurse was searching through her purse and looked at me surprised and annoyed, but my aunt was there beneath the light cover with her bird's profile, her mouth half-opened in the death-rattle, her eyelids yellow. I brushed her hand, she gave out a faint lament as if I had hurt her. "What are you doing?" the nurse scolded me while the dying woman groaned louder and already on the stairs a shuffling could be heard and the doctor appeared followed by a panting Ersilia. Then came Tommaso, Ferdinando, Antonio, Orazio, with intent sweating faces and wide eyes, trailing the smell of smoke. I lowered my head, made my way through them, went slowly down the stairs and into the kitchen. The two old women had fallen asleep at the table, their heads on their arms under the low lamp; the sink was full of little cups, plates. The doctor was coming down saying to Ersilia: "She won't see morning." I looked outside through the window, searching the shadows for an explanation, an answer, but I saw only shadows and red cigarette butts. Silent and relatively stable groups had formed and were seated at the little tables. Galileo was whining and calling softly to Ersilia, perhaps because he had to go to the bathroom. I shook one of the old women. The other awoke too and they looked at me for a second, uncomprehending. "Do we have to go up?" but I nudged them toward the old man fretting on the big chair, rubbing his hands on his skinny knees. "He has to go to the bathroom, could you take him please?"

But it is pointless going on like this, you see it too, it is pointless telling all these little details, they're not the right ones, I am losing myself again in the unsuspected geometries of those silent colonnades and I realize that I have told you nothing, even if a little came out about that night from the humid undergrounds, laboriously, through the reconstruction of these moments that reflect each other, magnified, in the flight of the years that have passed since then, in the dispersion along different paths of those who were there that night. And that resigned and nerve-wracking wait for what was, after all, a foreseen and almost obvious event moves now through distant, contiguous planes into the present, so that I feel with crumbling certainty that everything must happen again just as it happened so many times before. With imperceptible and exact progressions, time reaches back to that night whose every part sways and escapes around edges that open and reveal dusty cracks leading down to icy cellars where they fan into infinite and parallel edges. In the cyclic dreams that I nurture there are gluey cities full of missed appointments and anxious little streets where I can't find a common place for Galileo, Ferdinando, the aunt, and everything seems marked by an ephemeral constancy of time that pervades and always betrays, but each time a little less, until there is an exact convergence on a distant horizon to the hours of that night. And Gianna, who seems to me to be the only reason for living in the face of the deaths of the innumerable other worlds where I had long cherished dreams and bewilderments before arriving at this one, even Gianna wavers and eludes me and in all these dreams I follow her down incongruous half-dark streets where she always refuses to rest her cheek on my shoulder giving childish and tormenting excuses, and it doesn't matter that awaking I find her at my side breathing lightly in her sleep, because all is confused in that distant rustle, in that night that rolls up together the last breaths of the aunt, and Galileo in his big chair with his convulsive hands, and Ferdinando with his congested face who will try to reassure Enrichetta, poor withered and falling old maid, and the whole house, all the relatives who will arrive a few at a time greeting each other, cheerful and contrite.

And I return by dead-end streets within my dreams, and in the dark distances of an invisible countryside the whistles of the trains chase each other along infinite horizons and the gravel crunches under the feet of Antonio who again asks Ersilia for coffee and the two old women can finally go upstairs to wash the dead aunt, and the doctor with the swollen and defeated face looks for his bag while the dawn makes the roosters crow in the distance and illuminates everyone's decrepit faces and even Gianna's face frightens me, gray as it is with livid rings under her eyes, and I burst into convulsive tears and everyone watches me wordlessly chewing more and more slowly through the cigarette smoke that envelops them, and they come close and with patient surprise form a circle and I sobbing finally call my aunt and Gianna is there instead and I fall to my knees before her and kiss her hands weeping and she bends down to my eyes and with infinite sadness repeats no no with her head. All the relatives are around me and watch in sad wonder and already they are beginning to murmur and Enrichetta takes a step forward and immediately Ferdinando does the same right next to me and a dozen hands grasp me under the arms and pull me up and Antonio is motionless in a corner and watches his wife in front of me in her white dress, with her eyes wide in mine, her black hair gathered around her earthy face, her sorrowful mouth in the light that filters everywhere now like dirty water. And at those tears, at that uncontrollable convulsion of sobbing, Gianna with infinite patience turns on the light and caresses my face and forehead and says to me, no, my love, no, I am here, it is a bad dream and I turn and see her, with her half-closed eyes and her black and shining hair and hesitating I touch her and understand that that distant night is in another quadrant of time, and it filters through these openings in me and flows ever so slowly into these other nights, into this time and floods it, covers it in black, with a flaccid suffocating mucus, and I remain with gaping eyes looking around me while the past becomes the future again, and here again are those walls, the house, that countryside and outside the wind rustles and already the gravel crunches under the steps of Antonio, Orazio, Enrichetta, and of all the relatives who will come after dinner, if you can call dinner that distracted gulping of a couple of mouthfuls while straining our ears for noises upstairs.

Open City Index (Issues 1–25)

Bakowski, Peter. "The Width of the World," "We Are So Rarely Out of the Line of Fire" (poems). *Open City* 11 (2000): 95–100.

Balkenhol, Stephan. Drawings. *Open City* 5 (1997): 38–42.

Bar-Nadav, Hadara. "Talking to Strangers" (story). *Open City* 23 (2007): 11–23.

Bar-Nadav, Hadara. "Bricolage and Blood," "I Used to Be Snow White," "To Halve and to Hole" (poems). *Open City* 23 (2007): 25–29.

Bartók-Baratta, Edward. "Walker" (poem). *Open City* 18 (2003–2004): 175.

Baum, Erica. "The Following Information" (photographs). *Open City* 13 (2001): 87–94.

Baumbach, Jonathan. "Lost Car" (story). *Open City* 22 (2006): 27–35.

Baumbach, Nico. "Guilty Pleasure" (story). *Open City* 14 (2001–2002): 39–58.

Beal, Daphne. "Eternal Bliss" (story). *Open City* 12 (2001): 171–190.

Beatty, Paul. "All Aboard" (poem). *Open City* 3 (1995): 245–247.

Becker, Priscilla. "Blue Statuary," "Instrumental" (poems). *Open City* 18 (2003–2004): 151–152.

Becker, Priscilla. "Recurrence of Childhood Paralysis," "Blue Statuary" (poems). *Open City* 19 (2004): 33–34.

Becker, Priscilla. "Typochondria" (essay). *Open City* 22 (2006): 9–12.

Beckman, Joshua and Tomaz Salamun, trans., "VI," "VII" (poems) by Tomaz Salamun. *Open City* 15 (2002): 155–157.

Beckman, Joshua and Matthew Rohrer. "Still Life with Woodpecker," "The Book of Houseplants" (poems). *Open City* 19 (2004): 177–178.

Belcourt, Louise. "Snake, World Drawings" (drawings). *Open City* 14 (2001–2002): 59–67.

Bellamy, Dodie. "From *Cunt-Ups*" (poems). *Open City* 14 (2001–2002): 155–157.

Beller, Thomas. "Vas *Is* Dat?" (story). *Open City* 10 (2000): 51–88.

Bellows, Nathaniel. "At the House on the Lake," "A Certain Dirge," "An Attempt" (poems). *Open City* 16 (2002–2003): 69–73.

Bergman, Alicia. "Visit" (story). *Open City* 10 (2000): 125–134.

Berman, David. "Snow," "Moon" (poems). *Open City* 4 (1996): 45–48.

Berman, David. "Now, II," "A Letter From Isaac Asimov to His Wife, Janet, Written on His Deathbed" (poems). *Open City* 7 (1999): 56–59.

Berman, David. "Classic Water & Other Poems" (poems). *Open City* 5 (1997): 21–26.

Bernard, April. "Praise Psalm of the City Dweller," "Psalm of the Apartment Dweller," "Psalm of the Card Readers" (poems). *Open City* 2 (1993): 47–49.

Berne, Betsy. "Francesca Woodman Remembered" (story). *Open City* 3 (1995): 229–234.

Berrigan, Anselm. "'Something like ten million …'" (poem). *Open City* 14 (2001–2002): 159–161.

Brown, Jason. "North" (story). *Open City* 19 (2004): 1–19.

Brown, Lee Ann. "Discalmer" (introduction). *Open City* 14 (2001–2002): 137–139.

Brownstein, Michael. "The Art of Diplomacy" (story). *Open City* 4 (1996): 153–161.

Brownstein, Michael. "From *World on Fire*" (poetry). *Open City* 14 (2001–2002): 201–218.

Broyard, Bliss. "Snowed In" (story). *Open City* 7 (1999): 22–42.

Brumbaugh, Sam. "Safari Eyes" (story). *Open City* 12 (2001): 49–64.

Bukowski, Charles. "The Silver Christ of Santa Fe" (story). *Open City* 25 (2008): 63–68.

Bunn, David. "Book Worms" (card catalog art project). *Open City* 16 (2002–2003): 43–57.

Burton, Jeff. "Untitled #87 (chandelier)" (photograph). *Open City* 7 (1999): front cover.

Butler, Robert Olen. "Three Pieces of *Severance*" (stories). *Open City* 19 (2004): 189–191.

C, Mark. "What Calls Your Name" (photographs). *Open City* 25 (2008): 137–146.

Carter, Emily. "Glory Goes and Gets Some" (story). *Open City* 4 (1996): 125–128.

Carter, Emily. "Hampden City" (story). *Open City* 7 (1999): 43–45.

Cattelan, Maurizio. "Choose Your Destination, Have a Museum-Paid Vacation" (postcard). *Open City* 9 (1999): 39–42.

Cavendish, Lucy. "Portrait of an Artist's Studio" (drawings). *Open City* 11 (2000): 101–110.

Chamandy, Susan. "Hannibal Had Elephants with Him" (story). *Open City* 18 (2003–2004): 33–54.

Chan, Paul. "Self-Portrait as a Font" (drawings, text). *Open City* 15 (2002): 111–118.

Chancellor, Alexander. "The Special Relationship" (story). *Open City* 9 (1999): 189–206.

Charles, Bryan. "Dollar Movies" (story). *Open City* 19 (2004): 41–49.

Chase, Heather. "My First Facelift" (story). *Open City* 4 (1996): 23–44.

Chester, Alfred. "Moroccan Letters" (story). *Open City* 3 (1995): 195–219.

Chester, Craig. "Why the Long Face?" (story). *Open City* 14 (2001–2002): 109–127.

Chung, Brian Carey. "Still Life," "Traveling with the Lost" (poems). *Open City* 21 (2005–2006): 1153–156.

Clark, Joseph. "Nature Freak" (story). *Open City* 21 (2005–2006): 121–130.

Clements, Marcelle. "Reliable Alchemy" (story). *Open City* 17 (2003): 239–241.

Cohen, Elizabeth. "X-Ray of My Spine" (poem). *Open City* 2 (1993): 61–62.

Cohen, Marcel. "From *Letter to Antonio Saura*" (story), trans. Raphael Rubinstein. *Open City* 17 (2003): 217–225.

Dietrich, Bryan D. "The Thing That Couldn't Die" (poem). *Open City* 21 (2005–2006): 89–90.

Dikeou, Devon. Photographs, drawings, and text. *Open City* 1 (1992): 39–48.

Dikeou, Devon. "Marilyn Monroe Wanted to Be Buried In Pucci" (photographs, drawings, text,). *Open City* 10 (2000): 207–224.

Donnelly, Mary. "Lonely" (poem). *Open City* 12 (2001): 151–152.

Doris, Stacy. "Flight" (play). *Open City* 14 (2001–2002): 147–150.

Dormen, Lesley. "Gladiators" (story). *Open City* 18 (2003–2004): 155–163.

Douglas, Norman. "Male Order" (story). *Open City* 19 (2004): 151–163.

Dowe, Tom. "Legitimation Crisis" (poem). *Open City* 7 (1999): 21.

Doyle, Ben. "And on the First Day" (poem). *Open City* 12 (2001): 203–204.

Duhamel, Denise. "The Frog and the Feather" (story). *Open City* 5 (1997): 115–117.

Dyer, Geoff. "Albert Camus" (story). *Open City* 9 (1999): 23–38.

Grennan, Eamon. "Two Poems" (poems). *Open City* 5 (1997): 137–140.

Eisenegger, Erich. "A Ticket for Kat" (story). *Open City* 16 (2002–2003): 133–141.

Ellison, Lori. "Coffee Drawings" (drawings). *Open City* 13 (2001): 57–66.

Ellison, Lori. Drawing. *Open City* 17 (2003): back cover.

Ellman, Juliana. "Interior, Exterior, Portrait, Still-Life, Landscape" (drawings). *Open City* 19 (2004): 73–83.

Elsayed, Dahlia. "Black and Blue" (story). *Open City* 2 (1993): 29–35.

Elsayed, Dahlia. "Paterson Falls" (story). *Open City* 9 (1999): 153–158.

Engel, Terry. "Sky Blue Ford" (story). *Open City* 3 (1995): 115–128.

Eno, Will. "The Short Story of My Family" (story). *Open City* 13 (2001): 79–86.

Epstein, Daniel Mark. "The Jealous Man" (poem). *Open City* 17 (2003): 135–136.

Erian, Alicia. "Troika" (story). *Open City* 15 (2002): 27–42.

Erian, Alicia. "The Grant" (story). *Open City* 19 (2004): 109–117.

Eurydice. "History Malfunctions" (story). *Open City* 3 (1995): 161–164.

Faison, Ann. Drawings. *Open City* 12 (2001): 197–202.

Fattaruso, Paul. "Breakfast," "It Is I," "On the Stroke and Death of My Grandfather" (poems). *Open City* 20 (2005): 217–221.

Fawkes, Martin, trans., "Rehearsal for a Deserted City" (story) by Giuseppe O. Longo. *Open City* 15 (2002): 95–103.

Fernández de Villa-Urrutia, Rafael. "The First Visit to the Louvre: Fragments of an Improbable Dialogue" (story), trans. Jean Claude Abreu and Jorge Jauregui. *Open City* 16 (2002–2003): 177–181.

Field, Edward. Epilogue for Alfred Chester's "Moroccan Letters." *Open City* 3 (1995): 219.

Gersh, Amanda. "On Safari" (story). *Open City* 10 (2000): 135–150.

Gifford, William. "Fight" (story). *Open City* 4 (1996): 207–214.

Gilbert, Josh. "Hack Wars" (story). *Open City* 18 (2003–2004): 55–60.

Gillick, Liam. "Signage for a Four Story Building" (art project). *Open City* 8 (1999): 121–125.

Gillison, Samantha. "Petty Cash" (story). *Open City* 4 (1996): 197–206.

Ginsberg, Allen. Photograph and text. *Open City* 3 (1995): 191–194.

Gizzi, Peter. "Take the 5:01 to Dreamland" (poem). *Open City* 17 (2003): 151–152.

Gold, Herbert. "Next In Line" (story). *Open City* 22 (2006): 65–69.

Goldstein, Jesse. "Dance With Me Ish, Like When You Was a Baby" (story). *Open City* 17 (2003): 197–199.

Gonzalez, Manuel. "The Disappearance of the Sebali Tribe" (story). *Open City* 22 (2006): 49–64.

Gonzalez, Mark. "To You, My Reader" (story). *Open City* 8 (1999): 153–154.

Gonzalez, Wayne. "Interior, Exterior, Portrait, Still-Life, Landscape," "The Carousel Club," "Self-Portrait as a Young Marine" (paintings). *Open City* 19 (2004): 73–83; front and back covers.

Goodyear, Dana. "Things Get Better Before They Get Worse," "Oracle," "Séance at Tennis," "Setting" (poems). *Open City* 16 (2002–2003): 39–42.

Gorham, Sarah. "Bacchus at the Water Tower, Continuing Ed," "Middle Age" (poems). *Open City* 13 (2001): 111–114.

Gorham, Sarah. "The Sacrifice," "*Would you like to see the house?*" (poems). *Open City* 19 (2004): 119–121.

Gray, Peter. "Alley" (poem). *Open City* 16 (2002–2003): 183–184.

Green, Lohren. "From the *Poetical Dictionary*" (poem). *Open City* 16 (2002–2003): 129–132.

Greene, Daniel. "Paul's Universe Blue," "Mother, Worcester, 1953," "Learning to Stand" (poems). *Open City* 15 (2002): 43–47.

Grennan, Eamon. "Glimpse" (poem). *Open City* 17 (2003): 161.

Groebner, John. "The Fucker" (story). *Open City* 25 (2008): 161–168.

Grove, Elizabeth. "Enough About Me" (story). *Open City* 14 (2001–2002): 97–108.

Hakansson, Henrik. "Incomplete Proposals 1999–" (drawings). *Open City* 12 (2001): 89–94.

Hall, Marcellus. "As Luke Would Have It" (drawings, text). *Open City* 18 (2003–2004): 177–184.

Hannah, Duncan. Drawings. *Open City* 25 (2008): 169–176 and back cover.

Hannah, Duncan. "High Diver" (painting). *Open City* 25 (2008): front cover.

Hanrahan, Catherine. "The Outer-Space Room" (story). *Open City* 18 (2003-2004): 99–114.

Hoffman, Cynthia Marie. "Dear Commercial Street," (poem). *Open City* 17 (2003): 125–127.

Hofstede, Hilarius. "The Marquis Von Water" (text art project). *Open City* 3 (1995): 135–144.

Hogan, John Brinton. "Vacation" (photographs). *Open City* 20 (2005): 113–120.

Holland, J. Gill. Introduction to "The Journals of Edvard Munch." *Open City* 9 (1999): 229–232.

Holland, Noy. "Time for the Flat-Headed Man" (story). *Open City* 14 (2001–2002): 69–80.

Hollander, Katherine. "Snow Man" (poem). *Open City* 19 (2004): 187–188.

Howe, Fanny. "The Plan," "A Reach" (poems). *Open City* 17 (2003): 119–121.

Humphries, Jacqueline. Paintings. *Open City* 3 (1995): 235–244.

Hubby, Bettina. Illustrations for Susan Perry's "The Final Man." *Open City* 8 (1999): 15–171.

Iovenko, Chris. "The Turnaround" (story). *Open City* 5 (1997): 73–80.

Jack, Rodney. "Many Splendid Thing," "Mutually Exclusive" (poems). *Open City* 18 (2003–2004): 61–66.

Jack, Rodney. "From Nightlife" (story). *Open City* 23 (2007): 97–110.

Jack, Rodney. "Seedbed," "Black-Capped Chickadee Trapped in the Feeder," "Perpetuation" (poems). *Open City* 23 (2007): 111–114.

Jaramillo, Luis. "Jack and the Rotarians" (story). *Open City* 19 (2004): 85–91.

Jarnot, Lisa. "Self-Portrait" (poem). *Open City* 14 (2001–2002): 167.

Jauregui, Jorge and Jean Claude Abreu, trans., "The First Visit to the Louvre: Fragments of an Improbable Dialogue" (story) by Rafael Fernández de Villa-Urrutia. *Open City* 16 (2002–2003): 177–181.

John, Daniel. "The Diagnosis" (poem). *Open City* 19 (2004): 93.

Johnson, David. Image and text. *Open City* 3 (1995): 155–160.

Johnson, Denis. "An Anarchist's Guide to Somalia" (story). *Open City* 4 (1996): 89–116.

Johnson, Joyce. "Postwar" (story). *Open City* 8 (1999): 183–194.

Johnson, Marilyn A. "Her Deflowering" (poem). *Open City* 16 (2002–2003): 191.

Johnston, Bret Anthony. "Waterwalkers" (story). *Open City* 18 (2003–2004): 229–248.

Jones, Hettie. "5:15 p.m. Eastern Standard Time, November," "One Hundred Love Poems for Lisa" (poems). *Open City* 4 (1996): 86–88.

Jones, Sarah. "Dining Room (Francis Place) (III)" (photograph, detail). *Open City* 5 (1997): front cover.

Jones, Stephen Graham. "Bile" (story). *Open City* 14 (2001–2002): 81–88.

Kaplan, Janet. "The List" (poem). *Open City* 19 (2004): 71.

Kotzen, Kip. "Skate Dogs" (story). *Open City* 2 (1993): 50–53.

Kotzen, Kip. "Pray For Rain" (story). *Open City* 10 (2000): 159–170.

Kraman, Cynthia. "A Little Rock Memoir, Mostly About Other Things" (story). *Open City* 23 (2007): 125–133.

Kraman, Cynthia. "Little Gingko," "No Noon But Mine, No Heat But Yours," "Summer Night Poem 1," Summer Night Poem 5" (poems). *Open City* 23 (2007): 135–138.

Kujak, Heidi. "Father's Day," "San Francisco Produce Terminal" (poems). *Open City* 15 (2002): 109–110.

Lamb-Shapiro, Jessica. "This Man Is Eating in His Sleep" (story). *Open City* 17 (2003): 167–175.

Lambert, Alix. Untitled photographs. *Open City* 3 (1995): front cover and 34.

Lambert, Alix. "The Mark of Cain" (photographs, text). *Open City* 10 (2000): 183–194.

Lambert, Alix. "I am not like them at all and I cannot pretend" (collage). *Open City* 18 (2003–2004): 81–86.

Larimer, Heather. "Casseroles" (story). *Open City* 12 (2001): 75–88.

Larkin, Joan. "Full Moon Over Brooklyn" (poem). *Open City* 17 (2003): 123.

Larralde, Martin G. Paintings. *Open City* 11 (2000): 87–94.

Larson, Laura and Anne Trubek. "Genius Loci" (photographs, text). *Open City* 7 (1999): 85–94.

Larsson, Victoria. "Sharp Objects" (story). *Open City* 18 (2003–2004): 167–173.

Lasdun, James. "The Natural Order" (story). *Open City* 15 (2002): 201–221.

Lea, Creston. "We Used to Breed Remarkable Percheron Twitch Horses" (poem). *Open City* 12 (2001): 271.

Leckey, Mark. "The Casuals" (drawings, text). *Open City* 9 (1999): 119–128.

Leebron, Fred. "Welcome to Arcadia" (story). *Open City* 8 (1999): 111–119.

Legere, Phoebe. "Ode to Hong Kong" (poem). *Open City* 1 (1992): 23.

Lehman, David. "Eleven Poems for My Birthday" (poems). *Open City* 18 (2003–2004): 225–228.

Lehman, David. "Fast and Slow Sestina," "The Hotel Fiesta Sestina" (poems). *Open City* 20 (2005): 93–96.

LeMay, Patty. "confessions of a touring musician's lady (part 1)," "confessions of a touring musician's lady (part 24)" (poems). *Open City* 18 (2003–2004): 119–122.

Lesser, Guy. "The Good Sportsman, Et Cetera" (story). *Open City* 8 (1999): 75–86.

Levine, Margaret. "In a Dream It Happens," "Dilemma" (poems). *Open City* 16 (2002–2003): 159–160.

Lewinsky, Monica. "I Am a Pizza" (poem). *Open City* 6 (1998): 129.

Lewis, Jeremy. Introduction to "Happy Deathbeds." *Open City* 4 (1996): 49–52.

Masini, Donna. "3 Card Monte" (poem). *Open City* 17 (2003): 145–146.

Matthews, Richard. "Hudson" (poem). *Open City* 17 (2003): 107–108.

Maurer United Architects. "Façade" (photographs, images). *Open City* 15 (2002): 189–196.

Maxwell, Glyn. "Our Terrible Belief" (story). *Open City* 23 (2007): 139–148.

Maxwell, Glyn. "Sufficient Time," "Reality," "Decision," "Dust and Flowers," "The Arms of Half," "Fall of Man [Continued]" (poems). *Open City* 23 (2007): 149–156.

Maxwell, Richard. "A–1 Rolling Steak House" (play). *Open City* 13 (2001): 181–187.

McCabe, Patrick. "The Call" (story). *Open City* 3 (1995): 95–103.

McCormick, Carlo. "The Getaway" (story, drawings). *Open City* 3 (1995): 151–154.

McCracken, Chad. "Postcolonial Fat Man," "Second Grade" (poems). *Open City* 19 (2004): 165–167.

McCurtin, William. "Sometimes Skateboarding Is Like Dancing with Criminals" (drawings). *Open City* 20 (2005): 201–208.

McGuane, Thomas. "Bees" (story). *Open City* 4 (1996): 215–222.

McIntyre, Vestal. "Octo" (story). *Open City* 11 (2000): 27–50.

McIntyre, Vestal. "The Trailer at the End of the Driveway" (essay). *Open City* 22 (2006): 1–7.

McKenna, Evie. "Directions to My House" (photographs). *Open City* 12 (2001): 65–72.

McNally, John. "The First of Your Last Chances" (story). *Open City* 11 (2000): 125–140.

McNally, Sean. "Handsome Pants" (story). *Open City* 6 (1998): 131–132.

McPhee, Martha. "Waiting" (story). *Open City* 2 (1993): 109–118.

Mead, Stu. "Devil Milk" and "Untitled" (drawings). *Open City* 17 (2003): 177–185 and front cover.

Means, David. "What They Did" (story). *Open City* 6 (1998): 77–82.

Mehmedinovic, Semezdin. "Hotel Room," "Precautionary Manifesto" (poems), trans. Ammiel Alcaly. *Open City* 17 (2003): 141–142.

Mehta, Diane. "Rezoning in Brooklyn" (poem). *Open City* 7 (1999): 71–72.

Mendel, David, trans., "In Zenoburg" (story) by Giuseppe O. Longo. *Open City* 12 (2001): 153–160.

Mendel, David, trans., "Braised Beef for Three" (story) by Giuseppe O. Longo. *Open City* 19 (2004): 135–148.

Merlis, Jim. "One Man's Theory" (story). *Open City* 10 (2000): 171–182.

Metres, Philip and Tatiana Tulchinsky, trans., "This Is Me" (poem) by Lev Rubinshtein. *Open City* 15 (2002): 121–134.

Myles, Eileen. "Ooh" (poem). *Open City* 17 (2003): 143.

Myles, Eileen. "The Inferno" (story). *Open City* 18 (2003–2004): 67–74.

Nachumi, Ben. "Spring Cabin," "Crows," "Viking (to Calculus I)," "Dream House" (poems). *Open City* 21 (2005–2006): 71–76.

Nakanishi, Nadine. "Seriidevüf" (drawings). *Open City* 19 (2004): 122–128.

Nelson, Cynthia. "go ahead and sing your weird arias," "the adoration piles of spring," "i almost get killed" (poems). *Open City* 14 (2001–2002): 169–171.

Nelson, Maggie. "The Poem I Was Working on Before September 11, 2001" (poem). *Open City* 14 (2001–2002): 179–183.

Nester, Daniel. "After Schubert's Sad Cycle of Songs" (poem). *Open City* 15 (2002): 165–168.

Nevers, Mark. "Untitled" (poem). *Open City* 20 (2005): 121.

Newirth, Mike. "Semiprecious" (story). *Open City* 18 (2003–2004): 87–96.

Nutt, David. "Melancholera" (story) *Open City* 21 (2005–2006): 53–69.

O'Brien, Geoffrey. "Roof Garden" (poem). *Open City* 3 (1995): 134.

O'Brien, Geoffrey. "The Blasphemers" (story). *Open City* 5 (1997): 43–54.

O'Brien, Geoffrey. "House Detective" (poem). *Open City* 8 (1999): 120.

O'Brien, Geoffrey. "The Browser's Ecstasy" (story). *Open City* 10 (2000): 195–202.

O'Connor, John. "The Boil" (story). *Open City* 25 (2008): 147–160.

O'Rourke, Meg. "The Drivers" (story). *Open City* 2 (1993): 93–96.

Ogger, Sara, trans., "Show #7" (story) by Benjamin von Stuckrad-Barre. *Open City* 12 (2001): 119–130.

Okubo, Michiko. "The Glass Garden" (story). *Open City* 14 (2001–2002): 33–38.

Oldham, Will. "Untitled" (poem). *Open City* 7 (1999): 78.

Ortiz, Radames. "The Plea" (poem). *Open City* 18 (2003–2004): 211–212.

Osborne, Lawrence. "Gentle Toys" (story). *Open City* 4 (1996): 186–194.

Ovaldé, Véronique. "Scenes from Family Life" (story), trans. Lorin Stein. *Open City* 21 (2005–2006): 141–152.

Owens, Laura. Drawings *Open City* 9 (1999): 145–152.

Paco. "Clown Speaks" (story). *Open City* 2 (1993): 77–81.

Paco. "Clown White" (story). *Open City* 3 (1995): 103–110.

Paco. "Ing," "Cross and Sundial," "Flares," (stories), "Firecrackers and Sneakers" (poem). *Open City* 9 (1999): 219–226.

Pagk, Paul. Drawings. *Open City* 5 (1997): 89–98.

Panurgias, Basile. "The Sixth Continent" (story). *Open City* 5 (1997): 81–89.

Pape, Eric. "Faces of the Past and the Future" (essay). *Open City* 22 (2006): 13–25.

Passaro, Vince. "Cathedral Parkway" (story). *Open City* 1 (1992): 26–34.

Quinones, Paul. "Peter Gek" (story). *Open City* 15 (2002): 105–107.

Raffel, Dawn. "Seven Spells" (story). *Open City* 19 (2004): 181–185.

Raskin, Jimmy. Art project. *Open City* 2 (1993): 57–60.

Raskin, Jimmy. "The Diagram and the Poet" (text, image). *Open City* 7 (1999): 120–126.

Reagan, Siobhan. "Ambassadors" (story). *Open City* 5 (1997): 27–34.

Reagan, Siobhan. "Neck, 17.5" (story). *Open City* 11 (2000): 61–68.

Redel, Victoria. "The Palace of Weep" (poem). *Open City* 17 (2003): 153–154.

Reed, John. "Pop Mythologies" (story). *Open City* 2 (1993): 97–100.

Reising, Andrea. "LaSalle" (poem). *Open City* 11 (2000): 153–154.

Resen, Laura. Photographs. *Open City* 11 (2000): 145–152.

Reynolds, Rebecca. "Casper" (poem). *Open City* 15 (2002): 93–94.

von Rezzori, Gregor. "On the Cliff" (story). *Open City* 11 (2000): 199–240.

Richter, Jennifer. "Click," "Magic Word," "Recovery 2," "Relapse," "Recovery 4" (poems). *Open City* 25 (2008): 45–50.

Ricketts, Margaret. "Devil's Grass" (poem). *Open City* 11 (2000): 119.

Ritchie, Matthew. "$CaCO_2$" (drawings). *Open City* 6 (1998): 89–96.

Robbins, David. "Springtime" (photographs). *Open City* 8 (1999): 96–105.

Roberts, Anthony. "Wonders," "Two at Night," "Before Daybreak," "Beside the Orkhorn" (poems). *Open City* 20 (2005): 137–148.

Robertson, Thomas, and Rick Rofihe. "Four Round Windows" (drawings, text). *Open City* 19 (2004): 213–222.

Robinson, Lewis. "The Diver" (story). *Open City* 16 (2002–2003): 161–175.

Rofihe, Rick. "Eidetic," "'Feeling Marlene'" (stories). *Open City* 16 (2002–2003): 227–231.

Rofihe, Rick and Thomas Robertson. "Four Round Windows" (drawings, text). *Open City* 19 (2004): 213–222.

Rohrer, Matthew and Joshua Beckman. "Still Life with Woodpecker," "The Book of Houseplants" (poems). *Open City* 19 (2004): 177–178.

Ross, Sally. "Interior, Exterior, Portrait, Still-Life, Landscape" (drawings). *Open City* 19 (2004): 73–83.

Rothman, Richard. "Photographs" (photographs). *Open City* 6 (1998): 116–124.

Rubinshtein, Lev. "This Is Me" (poem), trans. Philip Metres and Tatiana Tulchinsky. *Open City* 15 (2002): 121–134.

Rubinstein, Raphael, trans., "From *Letter to Antonio Saura*" (story) by Marcel Cohen. *Open City* 17 (2003): 217–225.

Ruda, Ed. "The Seer" (story). *Open City* 1 (1992): 15.

Shapiro, Harvey. "Where I Am Now," "History," "How Charley Shaver Died" (poems). *Open City* 8 (1999): 23–25.

Shapiro, Harvey. "Places," "Epitaphs," "Cape Ann," "Confusion at the Wheel" (poems). *Open City* 11 (2000): 185–188.

Shapiro, Harvey. "One Day," "Night in the Hamptons" (poems). *Open City* 19 (2004): 209–211.

Shattuck, Jessica. "Winners" (story). *Open City* 21 (2005–2006): 1–12.

Shaw, Sam. "Peg" (story). *Open City* 20 (2005): 97–111.

Sherman, Rachel. "Keeping Time" (story). *Open City* 20 (2005): 81–91.

Sherman, Rachel. "Two Stories; Single Family; Scenic View" (story). *Open City* 21 (2005–2006): 77–88.

Shields, David. "Sports" (story). *Open City* 2 (1993): 119–120.

Shirazi, Kamrun. "Shirazi's Problem" (chess maneuvers). *Open City* 2 (1993): 128–129.

Shirazi, Said. "The Truce" (story). *Open City* 9 (1999): 107–116.

Shirazi, Said. "The Girl in the Fake Leopard-Skin Coat" (story). *Open City* 25: 85–98.

Shope, Nina. "Platform" (story). *Open City* 19 (2004): 55–61.

Siegel, Elke and Paul Fleming, trans., "December 24, 1999–January 1, 2000" (story) by Tim Staffel. *Open City* 12 (2001): 95–118.

Sigler, Jeremy. "Inner Lumber," "Obscuritea" (poems). *Open City* 20 (2005): 137–141.

Sirowitz, Hal. "Chicken Pox Story and Others" (poems, drawings). *Open City* 7 (1999): 73–77.

Skinner, Jeffrey. "Winn-Dixie," "Survey Says," "Video Vault" (poems). *Open City* 8 (1999): 69–74.

Sledge, Michael. "The Birdlady of Houston" (story). *Open City* 16 (2002–2003): 211–221.

Smith, Charlie. "A Selection Process," "Agents of the Moving Company," "Evasive Action" (poems). *Open City* 6 (1998): 43–46.

Smith, Lee. Two untitled poems. *Open City* 3 (1995): 224–225.

Smith, Lee. "The Balsawood Man" (story). *Open City* 10 (2000): 203–206.

Smith, Molly. "untitled (underlie)" (drawings). *Open City* 21 (2005–2006): 41–48.

Smith, Peter Nolan. "Why I Miss Junkies" (story). *Open City* 13 (2001): 115–129.

Smith, Peter Nolan. "Better Lucky Than Good" (story). *Open City* 19 (2004): 65–70.

Smith, Rod. "Sandaled" (poem). *Open City* 14 (2001–2002): 145.

Snyder, Rick. "No Excuse," "Pop Poem '98" (poems). *Open City* 8 (1999): 151–152.

Smith, Dean. "Head Fake" (poem). *Open City* 1 (1992): 19–20.

Smith, Scott. "The Egg Man" (story). *Open City* 20 (2005): 1–67.

Solotaroff, Ivan. "Love Poem (On 53rd and 5th)" (poem). *Open City* 3 (1995): 228.

Solotaroff, Ivan. "Prince of Darkness" (story). *Open City* 6 (1998): 97–114.

Thomas, Cannon. "Dubrovnik" (story). *Open City* 16 (2002–2003): 75–88.

Thompson, Jim. "Incident in God's Country" (story). *Open City* 4 (1996): 169–180.

Thomson, Mungo. "Notes and Memoranda" (drawings). *Open City* 12 (2001): 311–320.

Thomson, Mungo, curator. Art projects. *Open City* 16 (2002–2003).

Thorpe, Helen. "Killed on the Beat" (story). *Open City* 5 (1997): 118–136.

Torn, Anthony. "Flaubert in Egypt" (poem). *Open City* 1 (1992): 21–22.

Torn, Jonathan. "Arson" (story). *Open City* 1 (1992): 10–12.

Torn, Tony. "Hand of Dust," "Farmers: 3 a.m.," "To Mazatlan" (poems). *Open City* 10 (2000): 225–230.

Tosches, Nick. "My Kind of Loving" (poem). *Open City* 4 (1996): 23.

Tosches, Nick. "*L'uccisore e la Farfalla*," "*Ex Tenebris, Apricus*," "I'm in Love with Your Knees," "A Cigarette with God" (poems). *Open City* 13 (2001): 45–55.

Tosches, Nick. "Proust and the Rat" (story). *Open City* 16 (2002–2003): 223–226.

Tosches, Nick. "Gynæcology" (poem). *Open City* 18 (2003–2004): 165–166.

Tosches, Nick. "The Lectern at Helicarnassus" (poem). *Open City* 21 (2005–2006): 165.

Toulouse, Sophie. "Sexy Clowns" (photographs). *Open City* 17 (2003): 201–208.

Tower, Jon. Photographs, drawings, and text. *Open City* 1 (1992): 79–86.

Trubek, Anne and Laura Larson. "Genius Loci" (photographs, text). *Open City* 7 (1999): 85–94.

Tulchinsky, Tatiana and Paul Metres, trans., "This Is Me" (poem) by Lev Rubinshtein. *Open City* 15 (2002): 121–134.

Turner, Ben. "Composition Field 1," "Composition Field 2," "Soft-Core Porno" (poems). *Open City* 25: 123–130.

Uklanski, Piotr. "Queens" (photograph). *Open City* 8 (1999): front and back covers.

Uribe, Kirmen. "The River," "Visit" (poems) trans. Elizabeth Macklin. *Open City* 17 (2003): 131–134.

Vapnyar, Lara. "Mistress" (story). *Open City* 15 (2002): 135–153.

Vapnyar, Lara. "There Are Jews in My House" (story). *Open City* 17 (2003): 243–273.

Vicente, Esteban. Paintings. *Open City* 3 (1995): 75–80.

Vicuña, Cecilia. "The Brilliance of Orifices," "Mother of Pearl," "The Anatomy of Paper" (poems), trans. Rosa Alcalá. *Open City* 14 (2001–2002): 151–154.

Walker, Wendy. "Sophie in the Catacombs" (story). *Open City* 19 (2004): 131–132.

Wallace, David Foster. "Nothing Happened" (story). *Open City* 5 (1997): 63–68.

Walls, Jack. "Hi-fi" (story). *Open City* 13 (2001): 237–252.

Walser, Alissa. "Given" (story), trans. Elizabeth Gaffney. *Open City* 8 (1999): 141–150.

Walsh, J. Patrick III. "It's time to go out on your own." (drawings). *Open City* 19 (2004): 35–40.

Wolff, Rebecca. "Literary Agency," "My Daughter," "Only Rhubarb," "The Reductions," "Who Can I Ask for an Honest Assessment?" (poems). *Open City* 23 (2007): 239–243.

Woodman, Francesca. Untitled photographs. *Open City* 3 (1995): 229–234 and back cover.

Wormwood, Rick. "Burt and I" (story). *Open City* 9 (1999): 129–140.

Woychuk-Mlinac, Ava. "Why?" (poem). *Open City* 19 (2004): 179.

Yankelevich, Matvei, trans., "Who By Fire" (story) by Victor Pelevin. *Open City* 7 (1999): 95–106.

Yankelevich, M. E. Introduction to Daniil Kharms. *Open City* 8 (1999): 127–129.

Yankelevich, Matvei. "The Green Bench" (poem). *Open City* 19 (2004): 149–150.

Yas, Joanna. "Boardwalk" (story). *Open City* 10 (2000): 95–102.

Yates, Richard. "Uncertain Times" (unfinished novel). *Open City* 3 (1995): 35–71.

Yau, John. "Forbidden Entries" (story). *Open City* 2 (1993): 75–76.

Young, Kevin. "Encore," "Sorrow Song," "Saxophone Solo," "Muzak" (poems). *Open City* 16 (2002–2003): 121–127.

Zaitzeff, Amine. "Westchester Burning" (story). *Open City* 8 (1999): 45–68.

Zapruder, Matthew. "The Pajamaist" (poem). *Open City* 21 (2005–2006): 35–39.

Zumas, Leni. "Dragons May Be the Way Forward" (story). *Open City* 22 (2006): 15–22.

Zwahlen, Christian. "I Want You to Follow Me Home" (story). *Open City* 19 (2004): 27–32.